PIPPI IN THE SOUTH SEAS

But it was a real letter, a letter with many strange stamps.

"You read it, Tommy, you know how," said Pippi.

And Tommy began.

MY DEAR PIPPILOTTA, When you get this you might as well go down to the harbor and start looking for the Hoptoad. Because now I'm coming to get you and bring you here to Kurrekurredutt Island for a while. You ought at least to see the country where your father has become such a powerful king. It's really very nice here and I think that you would like it and feel at home. My faithful subjects are also looking forward very much to seeing the Princess Pippilotta of whom they have heard so much. So there is nothing further to be said in the matter. You are coming and this is my kingly and fatherly wish. A real big kiss and many fond regards from your old father,

KING EFRAIM I LONGSTOCKING
Ruler of Kurrekurredutt Island

When Tommy finished reading, you could have heard a pin drop in the kitchen.

OTHER PIPPI BOOKS YOU'LL ENJOY:

Pippi in the South Seas

ASTRID LINDGREN

Translated by Gerry Bothmer
Illustrated by Louis S. Glanzman

PUFFIN BOOKS

PUFFIN BOOKS

Published by the Penguin Group

Penguin Books USA Inc., 375 Hudson Street, New York, New York 10014, U.S.A.

Penguin Books Ltd, 27 Wrights Lane, London W8 5TZ, England

Penguin Books Australia Ltd, Ringwood, Victoria, Australia

Penguin Books Canada Ltd, 10 Alcorn Avenue, Toronto, Ontario, Canada M4V 3B2

Penguin Books (N.Z.) Ltd, 182-190 Wairau Road, Auckland 10, New Zealand

Penguin Books Ltd, Registered Offices: Harmondsworth, Middlesex, England

First published by The Viking Press, 1959
Viking Seafarer Edition published 1970
Reprinted 1972, 1973, 1974 (twice), 1975
First published in Puffin Books, 1977
This edition published in Puffin Books, 1997

56 57 58 59 60

ISBN 978-0-14-030958-4

Printed in the United States of America

Contents

Pippi in the South Seas

1
Villa
Villekulla

The little Swedish town was very picturesque, with its cobblestone streets, its tiny houses and the gardens that surrounded them. Everyone who visited there must have felt that this would be a calm and restful place to live. But as far as tourist attractions went, there wasn't much to see—almost nothing, in fact. There was a folklore museum, and an old grave mound, and that was all. But wait, there *was* one more thing!

The people of the little town had neatly and carefully put up signs to show visitors the way to the sights. To THE FOLKLORE MUSEUM was printed in large letters on one sign with an arrow underneath. To THE GRAVE MOUND read another sign.

There was still a third sign, saying, in rather crooked letters:

To Villa Villekulla

That sign had been put up quite recently. It had often happened lately that people would come and ask how to get to Villa Villekulla—as a matter of fact, more often than they would ask the way to the local museum or the grave mound.

One beautiful summer day a man came driving through the little town. He lived in a much bigger town and therefore he considered himself finer and more distinguished than the people who lived in smaller ones. Then, too, he had a very fine car and he was a very grand person, with shoes that were polished till they gleamed, and a thick gold ring on his finger. So it was perhaps not so strange that he thought of himself as fine and distinguished.

When he drove through the streets he honked his horn loudly so that everyone would notice him as he went by.

When the fine gentleman saw the signposts he laughed heartily.

To the Folklore Museum—how do you like that? he said to himself. I can do without that. *To the Grave Mound,* he read on the other sign. This is getting better and better. . . . But what sort of nonsense is this? he thought when he saw the third sign. *To Villa Villekulla*—what a name!

He thought about this for a moment. A villa could hardly be a tourist attraction in the same way that a folklore museum or a grave mound was. He decided that the sign must have been put there for another reason. Finally the answer came to him. The villa was of course for sale. The sign had been put up to show the way to people who might want to buy the house. For a long time he himself had been thinking that he would buy a house in a small town, where there was not so much noise as in the big city. Naturally he would not live there all the time, but he would go there to rest now and then. In a small town people would also be much more likely to notice what an unusually fine and distinguished man he really was. He decided to go and have a look at Villa Villekulla right away.

All he had to do was follow the direction of the arrow. But he had to drive to the edge of the town before he found what he was looking for. And there, printed with red crayon on a very broken-down garden gate, he read:

Villa Villekulla

Inside the gate was an overgrown garden with old trees covered with moss, and unmowed lawns, and lots of flowers which were allowed to grow exactly as they pleased. At the end of the garden was a house—and what a house! It looked as if it would fall to pieces any minute. The fine gentleman stared at it, and all of a sudden he groaned. A horse was standing on the veranda! The fine gentleman wasn't used to horses standing on verandas. That is why he groaned.

On the veranda steps three small children were sitting in the sunshine. The girl in the middle had lots of freckles on her face and two red pigtails which stuck straight out. A pretty blond curly-haired little girl in a blue checkered dress and a little boy with neatly combed hair sat one on either side of her. On the shoulder of the redheaded girl sat a monkey.

The fine gentleman was puzzled. He must have the wrong house. Surely no one would think there was a possibility of selling such a tumbledown shack?

"Listen, children," he called out to them, "is this miserable hovel really Villa Villekulla?"

The girl in the middle, the redheaded one, got up and came to the gate. The other two trudged slowly behind.

"Lost your tongue?" said the fine gentleman before the redheaded girl had reached him. "Is this shack Villa Villekulla?"

"Let me think," said the redheaded girl and frowned. "It isn't the museum and it isn't the grave

mound. *Now* I have it," she cried, "it *is* Villa Ville-kulla!"

"Don't be so rude," said the fine gentleman and got out of the car. He decided to take a closer look at the place. "I could of course tear this house down and build another one," he mumbled to himself.

"Yes, let's start right away!" cried the redheaded girl. She ran back to the house and briskly started to rip a few boards from the porch.

The fine gentleman paid no attention to her. He wasn't interested in children, and besides he now had something on his mind. The garden in its wild state really looked quite pleasant and attractive in the sunshine. If a new house were built, the lawns cut, the paths raked, and flowers properly planted, then even a very fine gentleman could live there. The fine gentleman decided to buy Villa Villekulla.

He looked around, trying to think of more ways to improve the place. Of course the old moss-covered trees would have to go. He glared sourly at the old gnarled oak with its tremendous trunk and its branches which arched over the roof of Villa Ville-kulla.

"I'll cut that one down," he said with finality.

The pretty little girl in the blue checkered dress cried out in a frightened voice, "Oh, Pippi, did you hear?"

Unconcerned, the redheaded girl continued to skip around on the garden path.

"Yes, I'll chop down that old rotten oak," the fine gentleman mumbled to himself.

The little girl in the blue checkered dress stretched her hands toward him pleadingly. "Oh, no, don't do that," she said. "It's such a wonderful tree to climb. And it's hollow, so we can play in it."

"Nonsense," said the fine gentleman. "I don't climb trees; you ought to understand that."

The boy with the neatly combed hair came forward. He looked anxious. "But soda grows in that tree," he said imploringly. "And chocolate too. On Thursdays."

"Listen, I think you kids have been sitting in the sun too long," said the fine gentleman. "Everything seems to be going round and round in your heads. But that's none of my business. I'm going to buy this place. Can you tell me where I can find the owner?"

The little blue checkered girl began to cry, and the little boy with the neatly combed hair ran up to the redheaded girl, who was still skipping. "Pippi," he said, "don't you hear what he is saying? Why don't you *do* something?"

"Why don't I *do* something?" echoed the redheaded girl. "Here I am, skipping for all I'm worth, and then you tell me I'm not doing anything. Skip yourself and see how easy it is!"

She walked over to the fine gentleman. "My name is Pippi Longstocking," she said. "And this is Tommy and Annika." She pointed to her friends. "Is there anything we can do for you—tear down a house or chop down a tree? Or is there anything else that needs to be changed? Just say the word!"

"Your names don't interest me," said the fine gentleman. "The only thing I would like to know is where I can find the owner of this place. I intend to buy it."

The redheaded girl, the one called Pippi Longstocking, had gone back to her skipping. "The owner is quite busy now," she said. She kept on skipping in a very determined way as she talked. "As a matter of fact, terribly busy," she said, skipping around the fine gentleman. "But do sit down and wait a while, and she will probably come along."

"*She*," said the fine gentleman with a pleased look. "Is it a *she* who owns this miserable house? So much the better. Women don't understand business. In that case there's a hope of getting it cheap."

"We can always hope," said Pippi Longstocking.

As there didn't seem to be any other place to sit down, the fine gentleman sat down on the veranda steps. The monkey anxiously leaped back and forth on the railing. Tommy and Annika were standing at a distance, looking at him in a frightened way.

"Do you live here?" asked the fine gentleman.

"No," said Tommy, "we live in the villa next door."

"But we come here every day to play," said Annika shyly.

"There will be an end to that now," said the fine gentleman. "I don't want any youngsters running around in my garden. Children are the worst thing I know."

"I think so too," said Pippi and stopped skipping for a second. "All children ought to be shot."

"How can you say that?" said Tommy, hurt.

"Yes, I mean it: all children ought to be shot," said Pippi. "But that isn't possible because then no nice little uncles would ever grow up. And we can't do without *them!*"

The fine gentleman looked at Pippi's red hair and decided to have a little fun while he was waiting. "Do you know why you're like a newly lighted match?" he asked.

"No," said Pippi. "But I have always wondered."

The fine gentleman pulled one of Pippi's pigtails quite hard. "Both of you are fiery on top—ha-ha!"

"One has to listen a lot before the ears fall off," said Pippi. "How strange that I haven't happened to think of that before!"

The fine gentleman looked at her and said, "I really think you're the ugliest child I've ever seen."

"Well," said Pippi, "you're not exactly a beauty yourself."

The fine gentleman looked hurt, but he didn't say anything. Pippi stood and looked at him in silence for a while with her head tilted to one side. "Do you know in what way you and I are alike?"

"Just between us," said the fine gentleman, "I hope there is *no* likeness."

"There is," said Pippi. "Both of us have big mouths. Except me."

A faint giggle could be heard from Tommy and Annika.

"So, you're being insolent!" the man shouted. "But I'll soon thrash that out of you."

He reached out his fat arm to grab Pippi, but she quickly jumped to one side and a second later she was sitting perched in the hollow oak. The fine gentleman gaped in astonishment.

"When are we going to start with the thrashing?" asked Pippi, as she made herself comfortable on a branch.

"I have time to wait," said the fine gentleman.

"Good!" said Pippi. "Because I'm thinking of staying up here until the middle of November."

Tommy and Annika laughed and clapped their hands. But that they shouldn't have done, because now the fine gentleman was terribly angry. When he couldn't reach Pippi he grabbed Annika by the nape of the neck and said, "Then I'll give you a hiding instead. It seems as if you need one too."

Annika had never in her life been spanked and she let out a cry of pain and fright. There was a thud as Pippi jumped out of the tree. With one leap she was standing beside the fine gentleman.

"Oh, no," she said. "Better not start a fight now." Then she grabbed the fine gentleman around his fat waist and threw him up in the air several times. And on her outstretched arms she carried him to his car and threw him down in the back seat.

"I think we'll wait to tear down the house until another day," she said. "You see, one day a week I tear down houses. But never on Fridays, because this is housecleaning day. Therefore I usually vacuum the house on Friday and tear it down on Saturday. Everything has its own time."

With great difficulty the fine gentleman scrambled up to the steering wheel and drove off in great haste. He was both frightened and angry and it annoyed him that he hadn't been able to talk to the owner of Villa Villekulla. He was anxious to buy the place and chase away those nasty children.

Then he met one of the town policemen. He stopped his car and said, "Can you help me to find the lady who owns Villa Villekulla?"

"With great pleasure," said the policeman. He hopped into the car and said, "Drive to Villa Villekulla."

"No, she isn't there," said the fine gentleman.

"Yes, I'm sure she's there," said the policeman.

The fine gentleman felt quite safe with the policeman along, and he drove back to Villa Villekulla as the policeman had told him to. He was very eager to talk to the owner.

"There is the lady that owns Villa Villekulla," said the policeman and pointed toward the house.

The fine gentleman looked in the direction in which the policeman was pointing. He put his hand to his forehead and groaned. There on the veranda steps was the redheaded girl, that awful Pippi Longstocking. And on her outstretched arms she was carrying the horse. The monkey was sitting on her left shoulder.

"Hi, Tommy and Annika," shouted Pippi, "let's go for a ride before the next spicalator comes!"

"It's called *speculator*," said Annika.

"Is that—the owner of the villa?" said the fine

gentleman in a weak voice. "But she is only a little girl."

"Yes," said the policeman, "only a little girl, the strongest little girl in the world. She lives there all alone."

The horse with the three children on his back came galloping toward the gate.

Pippi looked down at the fine gentleman and said, "It was fun to solve riddles with you a while ago. Come to think of it, I know one more. Can you tell me what the difference is between my horse and my monkey?"

The fine gentleman was really not at all in the mood to solve riddles any more, but he had gained so much respect for Pippi that he didn't dare not to answer.

"The difference between your horse and your monkey—that I really couldn't say."

"It's quite tricky," said Pippi, "but I'll give you a small hint. If you should see them both together under a tree and one of them should start to climb up the tree, then that one isn't the horse."

The fine gentleman pressed his gas pedal all the way down to the floor and took off with a roar. He never, never came back to the little town.

2
Pippi Cheers
Aunt Laura Up

One afternoon Pippi was wandering around in her garden, waiting for Tommy and Annika to come over. But no Tommy came, and no Annika either, so Pippi decided to go and see where they were. She found them in their own garden. But they weren't alone. Their mother, Mrs. Settergren, was also there with a very nice old lady who had come to visit. The two ladies were sitting under a tree, drinking coffee. Annika and Tommy were having fruit juice, but when they saw Pippi they got up and ran to meet her.

"Aunt Laura came," Tommy explained. "That's why we couldn't come over to you."

"She looks so nice," said Pippi, peeking at her through the leaves of the hedge. "I must talk to her. I'm so fond of nice old ladies."

Annika looked a little worried. "It . . . it . . . maybe it's best if you don't talk very much," she said. She remembered that once when Pippi had been to a coffee party she had talked so much that Annika's mother had been very annoyed with her. And Annika was too fond of Pippi to want anyone to be annoyed with her.

Pippi's feelings were hurt. "Why shouldn't I talk to her?" she asked. "When people come to visit, you should be nice and friendly to them. If I sit there and don't say a word, she might think I have something against her."

"But are you sure you know how to talk to old ladies?" objected Annika.

"They need to be cheered up," said Pippi with emphasis. "And that's what I'm going to do now." She walked across the lawn to where the two ladies were sitting. First she curtsied to Mrs. Settergren. Then she looked at the old lady and clapped her hands.

"Just look at Aunt Laura!" she exclaimed. "More beautiful than ever!" She turned to Tommy's and Annika's mother. "Please may I have a little fruit juice so my throat won't be so dry when we start talking?" she asked.

Mrs. Settergren poured a glass of juice and said as she handed it to Pippi, "Children should be seen and not heard."

"Well," said Pippi, looking pleased, "it's nice if

people are happy just to look at me! I must see how it feels to be used just for decoration." She sat down on the grass and stared straight in front of her with a fixed smile, as if she were having her picture taken.

Mrs. Settergren paid no further attention to Pippi but went on talking to the old lady. After a while she asked with concern, "How are you feeling these days, Aunt Laura?"

"Awful," replied Aunt Laura, "just awful. I'm so nervous and worried about everything."

Pippi jumped up. "Exactly like my grandmother!" she exclaimed. "She got nervous and excited about the least little thing. If she was walking in the street and a brick happened to fall on her head she'd start to scream and make such a fuss you'd think something terrible had happened.

"And once she was at a ball with my father and they were dancing a *hambo* together. My father is quite strong, and quick as a wink he swung my grandmother around so hard that she flew straight across the ballroom and landed with a crash right in the middle of the bass fiddle. There she was, screaming and carrying on like anything. My father picked her up and held her outside the window—it was four floors up—so that she'd cool off and not be so fidgety. But she didn't like that a bit. She just hollered, 'Let me go this minute!' My father did, of course, and can you imagine, she wasn't pleased about that either! My father said he'd never seen anything like the fuss the dear old lady made over nothing at all. It certainly is too bad when people have trouble with their nerves," Pippi finished sympathetically, and dunked her zwieback into her fruit juice.

Tommy and Annika were fidgeting uneasily in their chairs. Aunt Laura shook her head in a puzzled way, and Mrs. Settergren said hastily, "We all hope you'll be feeling better soon, Aunt Laura."

"Oh yes, I'm sure she will," Pippi said reassuringly. "My grandmother did. She was soon feeling very well."

Aunt Laura wanted to know what cured her.

"Tranquilizers," Pippi said. "That did the trick, I can tell you. She was soon as cool as a cucumber, and she'd sit peacefully for days at a time just not saying a word. If bricks had started falling on her head one after another she'd just have sat there and enjoyed it! If that could happen to my grandmother it could happen to *anybody*. So I'm sure you'll be all well again soon, Aunt Laura."

Tommy crept over to Aunt Laura and whispered

in her ear, "Don't mind anything Pippi says, Aunt Laura. She's just making it up. She doesn't even have a grandmother."

Aunt Laura nodded understandingly. But Pippi had sharp ears, and she heard what Tommy whispered.

"Tommy's quite right," she said. "I *don't* have a grandmother. She doesn't exist. Since that's the case, why does she have to be so terribly nervous?"

Aunt Laura looked at Pippi for a moment with a dazed expression, and then began to talk to Mrs. Settergren again. Pippi sat down to listen with the same fixed smile as before.

After a few minutes Aunt Laura said, "Do you know, something very strange happened yesterday—"

"But it couldn't be nearly as strange as what I saw the day *before* yesterday," Pippi said reassuringly. "I was riding in a train, and we were going along full speed when suddenly a cow came flying through the open window with a big suitcase hanging on her tail. She sat down in the seat across from me and began to look through the timetable to see what time we'd get to Falkoping. I was eating a sandwich—I had loads of sandwiches, some sausage and some smoked herring—and I thought she might be hungry, so I offered her one. She took a smoked herring one and swallowed it practically whole!"

Pippi fell silent.

"That was really *very* strange," said Aunt Laura politely.

"Yes, you'd go a long way before you'd find another cow as strange as that one," Pippi agreed. "Just imagine, she took a smoked herring sandwich when there were still lots of sausage ones left!"

Mrs. Settergren interrupted to ask Aunt Laura if she'd like some more coffee. She filled Aunt Laura's cup and her own, and poured more fruit juice for the children. "You were going to tell about the strange thing that happened yesterday," she reminded the old lady.

"Oh, yes," said Aunt Laura, beginning to look worried again.

"Speaking of strange things happening," Pippi broke in hastily, "you'll enjoy hearing about Agaton and Teodor. Once when my father's ship came into Singapore we needed a new able-bodied seaman, and we took on Agaton. He was seven feet tall and so thin that his bones rattled like a rattlesnake's tail when he moved. He had pitch-black hair that came down to his waist, and only one tooth. That tooth was all the bigger, though—it grew all the way down to his chin.

"My father thought Agaton was uglier than anyone should be, and at first he didn't want him on board. Only then he decided that Agaton might be useful to have around to scare any fierce wild horses into stampeding. Well, then we got to Hong Kong, and we needed another able-bodied seaman, so we got Teodor. They were as much alike as a pair of twins."

"That certainly was a strange coincidence!" exclaimed Aunt Laura.

"Strange?" said Pippi. "What was so strange about it?"

"That they looked so much alike," Aunt Laura replied. "That was very strange indeed."

"No," said Pippi, "not really. Because they *were* twins. Both of them. Even from birth." She looked a bit reproachful. "I don't quite understand what you mean, dear Aunt Laura. Is it anything to worry about when twins happen to look alike? They can't help it, you know. Nobody would have *wanted* to look like Agaton—or like Teodor either, for that matter."

"Then why do you speak of strange coincidences?" Aunt Laura asked, looking bewildered.

Mrs. Settergren tried to divert Aunt Laura's attention. "You were going to tell us about the strange thing that happened to you yesterday."

Aunt Laura got up to leave. "That will have to wait till another time," she said. "On second thought, perhaps it wasn't so very strange after all."

She said good-by to Tommy and Annika. Then she patted Pippi's red head. "Good-by, my little friend," she said. "You're quite right, I'm beginning to feel better already. I don't feel nervous at all any more."

"Oh, I'm so glad!" said Pippi, and gave the old lady a big hug. "You know, Aunt Laura, my father was very pleased about getting Teodor in Hong Kong. Because then he said he could stampede twice as many wild horses!"

3
Pippi
Finds
a Spink

One morning Tommy and Annika came skipping into Pippi's kitchen as usual, shouting good morning. But there was no answer. Pippi was sitting in the middle of the kitchen table with Mr. Nilsson, the little monkey, in her arms and a happy smile on her face.

"Good morning," said Tommy and Annika again.

"Just think," said Pippi dreamily, "just think that I have discovered it—I and no one else!"

"What have you discovered?" Tommy and Annika wondered. They weren't in the least bit surprised that Pippi had discovered something because she was always doing that, but they did want to know what it was.

"What did you discover, anyway, Pippi?"

"A new word," said Pippi and looked at Tommy and Annika as if she had just this minute noticed them. "A brand-new word."

"What kind of word?" said Tommy.

"A wonderful word," said Pippi. "One of the best I've ever heard."

"Say it then," said Annika.

"Spink," said Pippi triumphantly.

"Spink," repeated Tommy. "What does that mean?"

"If I only knew!" said Pippi. "The only thing I know is that it doesn't mean vacuum cleaner."

Tommy and Annika thought for a while. Finally Annika said, "But if you don't know what it means, then it can't be of any use."

"That's what bothers me," said Pippi.

"Who really decided in the beginning what all the words should mean?" Tommy wondered.

"Probably a bunch of old professors," said Pippi. "People certainly are peculiar! Just think of the words they make up—'tub' and 'stopper' and 'string' and words like that. Where they got them from, nobody knows. But a wonderful word like 'spink,' they don't bother to invent. How lucky that I hit on it! And you just bet I'll find out what it means, too."

She fell deep in thought.

"Spink! I wonder if it might be the top part of a blue flagpole," she said doubtfully.

"Flagpoles aren't blue," said Annika.

"You're right. Well, then, I really don't know.

. . . Or do you think it might be the sound you hear when you walk in the mud and it gets between your toes? Let's hear how it sounds! 'As Annika walked in the mud you could hear the most wonderful spink.'" She shook her head. "No, that's no good. 'You could hear the most wonderful *tjipp'*—that's what it should be instead."

Pippi scratched her head. "This is getting more and more mysterious. But whatever it is, I'm going to find out. Maybe it can be bought in the stores. Come on, let's go and ask!"

Tommy and Annika had no objection. Pippi went off to hunt for her purse, which was full of gold pieces. "Spink," she said. "It sounds as if it might be expensive. I'd better take a gold piece along." And she did. As usual Mr. Nilsson jumped up on her shoulder.

Then Pippi lifted the horse down from the veranda. "We're in a hurry," she said to Tommy and Annika. "We'll have to ride. Because otherwise there might not be any spink left when we get there. It wouldn't surprise me if the mayor had already bought the last of it."

When the horse came galloping through the streets of the little town with Pippi and Tommy and Annika on his back, the children heard the clatter of his hoofs on the cobblestones and came happily running because they all liked Pippi so much.

"Pippi, where are you going?" they cried.

"I'm going to buy spink," said Pippi and brought the horse to a halt for a moment.

The children looked puzzled.

"Is it something good?" a little boy asked.

"You bet," said Pippi and licked her lips. "It's wonderful. At least it sounds as if it were."

In front of a candy shop she jumped off the horse, lifted Tommy and Annika down, and in they went.

"I would like to buy a bag of spink," said Pippi. "But I want it nice and crunchy."

"Spink," said the pretty lady behind the counter, trying to think. "I don't believe we have that."

"You must have it," said Pippi. "All well-stocked shops carry it."

"Yes, but we've just run out of it," said the lady, who had never even heard of spink but didn't want to admit that her shop wasn't as well-stocked as any other.

"Oh, but then you did have it yesterday!" cried Pippi eagerly. "Please, please tell me how it looked. I've never seen spink in all my life. Was it red striped?"

Then the nice lady blushed prettily and said, "No, I really don't know what it is. In any case, we don't have it here."

Very disappointed, Pippi walked toward the door. "Then I have to keep on looking," she said. "I can't go back home without spink."

The next store was a hardware store. A salesman bowed politely to the children.

"I would like to buy a spink," said Pippi. "But I want it to be of the best kind, the one that is used for killing lions."

The salesman looked sly as a fox. "Let's see," he said and scratched himself behind the ear. "Let's see." He took out a small rake. "Is this all right?" he said as he handed it to Pippi.

Pippi looked indignantly at him. "That's what the professors would call a rake," she said. "But it happens to be a spink I wanted. Don't try to fool an innocent little child."

Then the salesman laughed and said, "Unfortunately we don't have the thing you want. Ask in the store around the corner that carries notions."

"Notions," Pippi muttered to Tommy and Annika when they came out on the street. "I just know they won't have it there." Suddenly she brightened. "Perhaps, after all, it's a sickness," she said. "Let's go and ask the doctor."

Annika knew where the doctor lived because she had gone there to be vaccinated.

Pippi rang the bell. A nurse opened the door.

"I would like to see the doctor," said Pippi. "It's a very serious case. A terribly dangerous disease."

"This way, please," said the nurse.

The doctor was sitting at his desk when the children came in. Pippi went straight to him, closed her eyes, and stuck her tongue out.

"What is the matter with you?" said the doctor.

Pippi opened her clear blue eyes and pulled in her tongue. "I'm afraid I've got spink," she said, "because I itch all over. And when I sleep my eyes close. Sometimes I have the hiccups and on Sunday I didn't feel very well after having eaten a dish of shoe polish and milk. My appetite is quite hearty, but sometimes I get the food down my windpipe and then nothing good comes of it. It must be the spink which bothers me. Tell me, is it contagious?"

The doctor looked at Pippi's rosy face and said, "I think you're healthier than most. I'm sure you're not suffering from spink."

Pippi grabbed him eagerly by the arm. "But there is a disease by that name, isn't there?"

"No," said the doctor, "there isn't. But even if there were, I don't think it would have any effect on you."

Pippi looked sad. She made a deep curtsy to the doctor as she said good-by, and so did Annika. Tommy bowed. And then they went out to the horse, who was waiting at the doctor's fence.

Not far from the doctor's house was a high three-story house with a window open on the upper floor. Pippi pointed toward the open window and said, "It wouldn't surprise me if the spink is in there. I'll dash up and see." Quickly she climbed up the water spout. When she reached the level of the window she threw herself heedlessly into the air and grabbed hold of the window sill. She hoisted herself up by the arms and stuck her head in.

In the room two ladies were sitting chatting. Imagine their astonishment when all of a sudden a red head popped over the window sill and a voice said, "Is there by any chance a spink here?"

The two ladies cried out in terror. "Good heavens, what are you saying, child? Has someone escaped?"

"That is exactly what I would like to know," said Pippi politely.

"Maybe he's under the bed!" screamed one of the ladies. "Does he bite?"

"I think so," said Pippi. "He's supposed to have tremendous fangs."

The two ladies clung to each other. Pippi looked around curiously, but finally she said with a sigh,

"No, there isn't as much as a spink's whisker around here. Excuse me for disturbing you. I just thought I would ask, since I happened to be passing by."

She slid down the water spout and said sadly to Tommy and Annika, "There isn't any spink in this town. Let's ride back home."

And that's what they did. When they jumped down from the horse outside the veranda, Tommy came close to stepping on a little beetle which was crawling on the gravel path.

"Be careful not to step on the beetle!" Pippi cried.

All three bent down to look at it. It was such a tiny thing, with green wings that gleamed like metal.

"What a pretty little creature," said Annika. "I wonder what it is."

"It isn't a June bug," said Tommy.

"And no ladybug either," said Annika. "And no stagbeetle. I wish I knew what it was."

All at once a radiant smile lit up Pippi's face. "I know," she said. "It's a spink."

"Are you sure?" Tommy said doubtfully.

"Don't you think I know a spink when I see one?" said Pippi. "Have you ever seen anything so spink-like in your life?"

She carefully moved the beetle to a safer place, where no one could step on it. "My sweet little spink," she said tenderly. "I knew that I would find one at last. But isn't it funny! We've been hunting all over town for a spink, and here was one right outside Villa Villekulla all the time!"

4
Pippi Arranges a Question-and-Answer Bee

The long wonderful summer holiday suddenly came to an end, and Tommy and Annika went back to school. Pippi still considered herself sufficiently well educated without going to school and announced very decidedly that she had no intention of setting her foot in school until the day came when she couldn't stand not knowing how the word "seasick" was spelled.

"But since I'm never seasick I don't have to worry about the spelling in the first place," she said. "And *if* I should happen to be seasick one day, then I'll have other things to think about than knowing how to spell it."

"Besides, you'll probably never get seasick," said Tommy.

And he was right. Pippi had sailed far and wide with her father before he became king of a South Sea island and before Pippi had settled down to live in Villa Villekulla. But in all her life she had never been seasick.

Sometimes Pippi would ride over and pick up Tommy and Annika when school was over. This pleased Tommy and Annika very much. They loved to ride, and there certainly aren't many children who are able to ride home from school on horseback.

"Please, Pippi, come and pick us up this afternoon," said Tommy one day just as he and Annika were going to dash back to school after their lunch hour.

"Yes, please," said Annika. "Because today is the day that Miss Rosenblom is going to give out gifts to children who have been good and worked hard."

Miss Rosenblom was a rich old lady who lived in the little town. She took good care of her money, but once every term she came to school and distributed gifts to the children. But not to all the children—oh, no! Only the very good and hard-working children got presents. To make sure she would know which children were really good and hard-working, Miss Rosenblom held long examinations before she distributed the presents. That was the reason all the children in town lived in constant dread of her. Every day when they were about to do their homework and were trying to think of something more amusing to do before getting started, their mother or father would say, "Remember Miss Rosenblom!"

It was a terrible disgrace to come home to one's parents and brothers and sisters the day Miss Rosenblom had been to school, and not have a small coin or bag of candy or at least some underwear to show for it. Yes, of all things, underwear! Because Miss Rosenblom distributed underwear to the poorest children. But it didn't matter how poor a child was if he didn't know the answer when Miss Rosenblom asked how many inches there were in a mile. It wasn't surprising at all that the children were afraid of Miss Rosenblom!

They lived in terror of her soup too. Believe it or not, Miss Rosenblom had all the children weighed and measured in order to see if there were any among them who were especially thin and pathetic and who looked as if they weren't getting enough to eat at home. All those who were found to be poor and too skinny had to go to Miss Rosenblom's every lunch hour and eat a big plate of soup. It would have been fine if there hadn't been a whole lot of nasty barley in the soup. It always felt so slippery in the mouth.

Now the big day had arrived when Miss Rosenblom was coming to the school. Classes stopped earlier than usual, and all the children gathered in the school yard. Miss Rosenblom sat at a big table that had been placed in the middle of the yard. To help her, she had two assistants who wrote down everything about the children—how much they weighed, if they were able to answer her questions, if they were poor and needed clothes, if they had good marks in conduct, if they had younger brothers and sisters at home who also needed clothing. There was no end to the things that Miss Rosenblom wanted to know. A box containing coins stood on the table in front of her. There were also a lot of bags of candy, and big piles of undershirts and socks and woolen pants.

"All children get in line!" shouted Miss Rosenblom. "In the first line I want children who don't have brothers and sisters at home; in the second line children who have one or two brothers and sisters; and in the third, children who have more than two brothers and sisters." This arrangement was made because Miss Rosenblom wanted everything to be orderly. Besides, it was only fair that the children who had many brothers and sisters at home should get bigger bags of candy than those who didn't have any.

Then the examination began. Oh, how the children trembled! The ones who couldn't answer the minute a question was asked had to go and stand in a corner, and then they were sent home without as much as one piece of candy for their little brothers and sisters.

Both Tommy and Annika were very good at their school work. But in spite of that, the bow in Annika's hair quivered with suspense as she stood in line beside Tommy. And Tommy's face got whiter and whiter the closer he got to Miss Rosenblom. When it was his turn to answer there was a sudden commotion in the line for children without brothers and sisters. Someone was pushing her way forward through the crowd, and who should it be but Pippi! She brushed the children aside and went straight up to Miss Rosenblom.

"Excuse me, but I wasn't here when you started," she said. "In which line should I stand, since I don't have fourteen brothers and sisters of which thirteen are naughty little boys?"

Miss Rosenblom looked very disapproving. "You can stay where you are for the present," she said. "But it seems to me that quite soon you will be moved over into the line of children who are going to stand in the corner."

Then the assistants wrote down Pippi's name and she was weighed in order to find out whether she needed any soup. But she weighed five pounds too much for that.

"You don't get any soup," said Miss Rosenblom sharply.

"Sometimes luck is with me," said Pippi. "Now all I have to do is get by without getting stuck with the underwear. Then I'll be able to breathe more freely."

Miss Rosenblom paid no attention to her. She was looking through the dictionary for a difficult word for Pippi to spell.

"Now then," she said finally, "will you tell me how you spell 'seasick'?"

"I'll be glad to," said Pippi. "S-e-e-s-i-k."

Miss Rosenblom smiled—a sour smile. "Is that so?" she said. "The dictionary spells it differently."

"Then it was very lucky that you wanted to know how *I* spell it," said Pippi. "S-e-e-s-i-k is the way I have always spelled it, and it seems to have worked out just fine."

"Make a note of that," said Miss Rosenblom to the assistants and grimly pressed her lips together.

"Yes, do that," said Pippi. "Make a note of this fine spelling and see to it that the change is made in the dictionary as soon as possible."

"I wonder if you can answer this one," said Miss Rosenblom. "When did King Charles the Twelfth die?"

"Oh dear, is he dead too?" cried Pippi. "It's awful

how many people die these days! If he had kept his feet dry I'm sure it would never have happened."

"Make a note of that," said Miss Rosenblom to her assistants in an icy voice.

"Yes, by all means do that," said Pippi. "And make a note that it's very good to keep leeches next to the skin. And you should drink a little warm kerosene before going to bed. It's very invigorating!"

Miss Rosenblom looked desperate. "Why does a horse have molars with dark markings running through them?" she asked in a stern voice.

"But are you sure that he has?" said Pippi thoughtfully. "You can ask him yourself. He is standing over there," she said and pointed to her horse, who was tied to a tree. She laughed contentedly. "It's a good thing I brought him along," she said. "Otherwise you would never have known why he has molars with markings in them. Because honestly I have no idea—and, what's more, I don't care much either."

A narrow line was now all that was left of Miss Rosenblom's mouth. "This is unbelievable," she murmured, "absolutely unbelievable."

"Yes, I think so too," said Pippi, pleased. "If I continue being this clever, I probably won't be able to avoid getting a pair of pink woolen underdrawers."

"Make a note of that," said Miss Rosenblom to the assistants.

"No, don't bother," said Pippi. "I really don't care so much about pink woolen underdrawers. That wasn't what I meant. But you could make a note saying I'm to have a big bag of candy."

"I'm going to ask you one more question," said Miss Rosenblom, and her voice sounded as if she were strangling.

"Yes, keep right on," said Pippi. "I like this kind of question-and-answer game."

"Can you answer this one?" said Miss Rosenblom. "Peter and Paul are going to divide a cake. If Peter gets one fourth, what does Paul get?"

"A stomach-ache," said Pippi. She turned to the assistants. "Make a note of that," she said seriously. "Make a note that Paul gets a stomach-ache."

But Miss Rosenblom was finished with Pippi. "You are the most stupid and disagreeable child I have ever seen," she said. "Go over and stand in the corner right away!"

Pippi obediently trotted off, muttering angrily to herself, "It's unfair, because I answered every question!" When she had walked a few steps she suddenly thought of something and quickly elbowed her way back to Miss Rosenblom.

"Excuse me," she said, "but I forgot to give my chest measurement and my height above sea level. Make a note of that," she said to the assistants. "Not that I want any soup—far from it—but the books should be in order, after all."

"If you don't go over and stand in the corner immediately," said Miss Rosenblom, "I know a little girl who is going to get a sound spanking."

"Poor child," said Pippi. "Where is she? Send her to me and I'll defend her. Make a note of that."

Then Pippi went over and stood in the corner with the children who couldn't answer questions. There the atmosphere was far from gay. Many of the children were sobbing and crying at the thought of what their parents and their brothers and sisters would say when they came home without the least little coin and without any candy.

Pippi looked around at the crying children and swallowed hard several times. Then she said, "We'll have a question-and-answer bee all our own!"

The children looked a bit more cheerful, but they didn't quite understand what Pippi meant.

"Form two lines," said Pippi. "All of you who know that King Charles the Twelfth is dead stand in one line and those who still haven't heard that he is dead stand in the other."

But since all the children knew that Charles the Twelfth was dead there was only one line.

"This is no good," said Pippi. "You have to have at least two lines, otherwise it isn't right. Ask Miss Rosenblom and you'll see." She stopped to think. "I have it!" she said at last. "All very clever and well-trained pranksters will form one line."

"And who is to stand in the other line?" a little girl who didn't want to be thought of as a prankster asked eagerly.

"In the other line we'll put all those who are not quite so clever at playing pranks," said Pippi.

Over at Miss Rosenblom's table the questioning was continuing full force and now and then a child on the verge of tears came shuffling over to Pippi's crowd.

"And now comes the hard part," said Pippi. "Now we're going to see if you have been doing your homework." She turned to a skinny little boy in a blue shirt. "You over there," she said, "give me the name of someone who is dead."

The boy looked a little surprised, but then he said, "Old Mrs. Pettersson in Number Fifty-seven."

"What do you know?" said Pippi. "Do you know anyone else?"

No, the boy didn't. Then Pippi put her hands in

front of her mouth in the form of a megaphone and said in a stage whisper, "King Charles the Twelfth, of course!"

Then Pippi asked all the children in turn if they knew anyone who was dead, and they all answered, "Old Mrs. Pettersson in Number Fifty-seven and King Charles the Twelfth."

"This examination is going better than I had expected," said Pippi. "Now I'm going to ask only one thing more. If Peter and Paul are going to divide a cake, and Peter absolutely doesn't want any but sits himself down in a corner and gnaws on a dry little bit of bread, who is then forced to sacrifice himself and down the whole cake?"

"Paul!" shouted all the children.

"I wonder if children as clever as you could be found anywhere else," said Pippi. "But you shall have a reward."

From her pockets she dug out a whole handful of gold pieces and each child got one. Each child also got a huge bag of candy, which Pippi took out of her rucksack.

That is why there was great rejoicing among the children who were supposedly in disgrace. And when Miss Rosenblom's examination was finished and everybody was going home, the children who had been standing in the corner were the quickest to disappear. But first they all crowded around Pippi.

"Thank you, dear Pippi," they said. "Thank you for the gold pieces and the candy."

"It's nothing," said Pippi. "You don't need to thank me. But you must never forget that I rescued you from the pink woolen underdrawers."

5
Pippi
Gets
a Letter

The days went by, and all of a sudden it was autumn—first autumn and then winter, a long, cold winter that seemed as if it would never end. Tommy and Annika were very busy at school, and with every day that went by they felt more tired and had a harder time getting up in the morning. Mrs. Settergren began to be really worried about their paleness and their lack of appetite. On top of everything, both of them suddenly caught the measles and had to stay in bed for a couple of weeks.

It would have been two very dreary weeks indeed if Pippi hadn't come and done tricks outside their window every day. The doctor had forbidden her to go into the sickroom, because measles are catching, and Pippi obeyed, although she said she would undertake to crack one or two billion measle microbes between her fingernails during the course of an afternoon.

But no one had forbidden her to do tricks outside the window. The children's room was on the second floor, and Pippi had raised a ladder to their window. It was very exciting for Tommy and Annika to lie in their beds and try to guess how Pippi would look when she appeared on the ladder, because she never looked the same two days in a row. Sometimes she would be dressed as a chimney sweep, sometimes as a ghost in a white sheet, and sometimes she appeared as a witch. Then she would act amusing skits outside the window, playing all the parts herself. Now and then she did acrobatics on the stepladder—and what acrobatics! She would stand on the topmost rung and let the ladder sway forth and back until Tommy and Annika screamed in terror because it looked as if she would come crashing down any minute. But she didn't. When she was going to climb down again she always went head first just so that it would be more amusing for Tommy and Annika to watch.

Every day she went to town to buy apples and oranges and candy. She put everything into a basket and attached it to a long string. Then Mr. Nilsson climbed up with the string to Tommy, who opened the window and hoisted up the basket. Sometimes Mr. Nilsson would also bring letters from Pippi when she was busy and couldn't come herself. But that didn't happen often, because Pippi was on the ladder practically all the time. Sometimes she pressed her nose against the windowpane and turned her eyelids inside out and made the most terrible faces. She said to Tommy and Annika that she would give each of them a gold piece if they could keep from laughing at her. But of course they couldn't. They laughed so hard that they almost fell out of their beds.

Gradually they became well again and were allowed to get up. But, oh, how pale and thin they were! Pippi was sitting with them in their kitchen the first day they were up, watching them eat their cereal. That is, they were supposed to be eating cereal, but they weren't doing very well. It made their mother terribly nervous to see them just sitting there and picking at it.

"Eat your good cereal," she said.

Annika stirred hers around in the dish with her spoon a bit, but she knew that she just couldn't get any of it down. "Why do I have to eat it, anyway?" she said complainingly.

"How can you ask anything so stupid?" said Pippi. "Of course you have to eat your good cereal. If you don't eat your good cereal, then you won't grow and get big and strong. And if you don't get big and strong, then you won't have the strength to force *your* children, when you have some, to eat *their* good cereal. No, Annika, that won't do. Nothing but the most terrible disorder in cereal-eating would come of this if everyone talked like you."

Tommy and Annika ate two spoonfuls of cereal each. Pippi watched them with great sympathy.

"You ought to go to sea for a while," she said, rocking back and forth on the chair on which she was sitting. "Then you would soon learn how to eat. I remember once when I was on my father's ship and Fridolf, one of our able-bodied seamen, suddenly one morning couldn't eat more than seven plates of cereal. My father was beside himself with worry over his poor appetite. 'Fridolf, old boy,' he said in a choked voice, 'I'm afraid that you have got a terrible, consuming disease. It's best that you stay in your bunk today, until you feel a little better and can eat normally. I'm coming back to tuck you in and give you some strengthening meducine.'"

"It's called *medicine*," said Annika.

"And Fridolf staggered to bed," Pippi went on, "because he was worried himself and wondered what sort of epidemic he could be having since he was only able to eat seven helpings of cereal. He was just lying there wondering whether he would live until evening when my father came with the meducine. A black, disgusting-looking meducine it was, but you could say what you wanted about it, it was strengthening. Because when Fridolf had swallowed the first spoonful, flames broke out from his mouth. He let out a scream that shook the *Hoptoad* from the stern to the bow and could be heard on ships within a fifty-mile radius.

"The cook still hadn't had a chance to clear away the breakfast dishes when Fridolf came steaming up into the galley, letting out piercing shrieks. He heaved himself down at the table and began eating cereal and he was howling with hunger even after his fifteenth plate. But then there was no more cereal left, and all the cook could do was stand and throw cold potatoes into Fridolf's open mouth. As soon as it looked as if he were going to stop, Fridolf let out an angry growl, and the cook realized that if he didn't want to be eaten up himself, all he could do was keep it up. But unfortunately he only had a miserable hundred and seventeen potatoes, and when he had thrown the last one into Fridolf's gullet he quickly made a dash for the door and turned the lock.

"Then we all stood outside and peeked in at Fridolf through a window. He was whining like a hungry child, and in quick succesion he ate up the bread basket and the pitcher and fifteen plates. Then he attacked the table. He broke off all four legs and ate till the sawdust foamed around his mouth, but he only said that for asparagus they had an awfully wooden taste. He seemed to think that the table top tasted better, because he smacked his lips as he ate it and said that it was the best sandwich he had eaten since he was a child. But then my father felt that Fridolf was fully recovered from his consuming disease, and he went in to him and said that now he would have to try to control himself until lunch, which would be served in two hours, and then he would get mashed turnips with salt pork. 'Oh, Captain!' said Fridolf, wiping his mouth. 'Please,' he said with an eager, hungry look in his eyes, 'when is supper going to be served and why can't we have it a little earlier?' "

Pippi put her head to one side and looked at Tommy and Annika and their cereal plates. "As I said, you ought to go to sea for a while and then your poor appetites would be cured in a hurry."

Just then the mailman walked by the Settergren house on his way to Villa Villekulla. He happened to see Pippi through the window and called out, "Pippi Longstocking, here is a letter for you!"

Pippi was so astonished that she almost fell off the chair. "A letter! For me? A leal retter—I mean, a real letter? I want to see it before I believe it."

But it *was* a real letter, a letter with many strange stamps.

"You read it, Tommy, you know how," said Pippi. And Tommy began.

My Dear Pippilotta, *When you get this you might as well go down to the harbor and start looking for the* Hoptoad. *Because now I'm coming to get you and bring you here to Kurrekurredutt Island for a while. You ought at least to see the country where your father has become such a powerful king. It's really very nice here and I think that you would like it and feel at home. My faithful subjects are also looking forward very much to seeing the Princess Pippilotta of whom they have heard so much. So there is nothing further to be said in the matter. You are coming and this is my kingly and fatherly wish. A real big kiss and many fond regards from your old father,*

King Efraim I Longstocking
Ruler of Kurrekurredutt Island

When Tommy had finished reading, you could have heard a pin drop in the kitchen.

6
Pippi Goes
on Board

On a beautiful morning the *Hoptoad* sailed into the harbor decorated with flags and pennants from end to end. The town band was on the pier, playing welcome songs with all its might. The whole town had gathered to see Pippi receive her father, King Efraim I Longstocking. A photographer was standing ready to snap a picture of their meeting.

Pippi was jumping up and down with impatience and the gangplank was hardly down before Captain Longstocking and Pippi rushed toward each other with shouts of joy. Captain Longstocking was so happy to see his daughter that he threw her way up in the air several times. Pippi was just as happy, so she threw her father way up in the air still more times. The only one who wasn't happy was the photographer, because he couldn't get a picture when either Pippi or her father was way up in the air all the time.

Tommy and Annika also came forward and greeted Captain Longstocking—but oh, how pale and miserable they looked! It was the first time after their illness that they had been out.

Pippi of course had to go on board and say hello to Fridolf and all her other friends among the seamen. Tommy and Annika trotted along too. They felt so strange walking around on a ship that had come from so far away, and they kept their eyes wide open so as not to miss anything. They were especially eager to see Agaton and Teodor, but Pippi said that the twins had signed off the ship a long time ago.

Pippi hugged all the sailors so hard that five minutes later they were still gasping for breath. Then she lifted Captain Longstocking up onto her shoulders and carried him through the crowd and all the way home to Villa Villekulla. Hand in hand, Tommy and Annika trudged along behind them.

"Long live King Efraim!" shouted all the people. They felt that this was a big day in the history of the little town.

A few hours later Captain Longstocking was in bed at Villa Villekulla, sleeping, and snoring away so that the whole house shook. Pippi, Tommy, and Annika were sitting around the kitchen table, where the remains of a splendid supper were still in evidence. Tommy and Annika were quiet and thoughtful. What were they thinking about? Annika was just thinking that when you come right down to facts, she would much rather be dead. Tommy was sitting there trying to remember if there was anything in this world that was really fun, but he couldn't think of a thing. Life was an empty waste, he felt.

But Pippi was in a wonderful mood. She stroked Mr. Nilsson, who was carefully making his way back and forth between the plates on the table; she stroked Tommy and Annika; she whistled and sang alternately and took happy little dance steps now and then. She didn't seem to notice that Tommy and Annika were so downcast.

"Going to sea for a bit again is going to be marvelous," she said. "Just think of being on the ocean, where there is so much freedom!"

Tommy and Annika sighed.

"And I'm quite excited about seeing Kurrekurredutt Island too. Imagine what it'll be like to lie stretched out on the beach, dipping my big toes in the South Pacific, and all I'll have to do is to open my mouth and a ripe banana will fall right in it!"

Tommy and Annika sighed.

"It's going to be a lot of fun to play with the children down there," Pippi continued.

Tommy and Annika sighed.

"What are you sighing for?" said Pippi. "Don't you like the idea of my playing with the native children?"

"Of course," said Tommy. "But we're just thinking that it will probably be a long time before you come back to Villa Villekulla."

"Yes, I'm sure of that," said Pippi gaily. "But I'm not at all sorry. I think I can have almost more fun on Kurrekurredutt Island."

Annika turned a pale, unhappy face toward Pippi. "Oh, Pippi," she said, "how long do you think you'll stay away?"

"Oh, that's hard to say. Until around Christmas, I should think."

Annika let out a wail.

"Who knows," said Pippi, "maybe I'll like it so much on Kurrekurredutt Island that I'll feel like staying there forever. . . . Tra-la-la," she sang, and did a few more pirouettes. "To be a princess, that's not a bad job for someone who's had as little schooling as I have."

Tommy's and Annika's eyes, looking out of their pale faces, began to have a peculiar, glassy stare. Suddenly Annika bent down over the table and burst into tears.

"But come to think of it, I don't think that I'd like

to stay there forever," said Pippi. "One can have too much of court life and get sick of the whole business. So one fine day you'll probably hear me saying, 'Tommy and Annika, how would you like to go back to Villa Villekulla for a while again?' "

"Oh, how wonderful it will be when you write that to us," said Tommy.

"*Write!*" said Pippi. "You have ears, I hope. I have no intention of writing. I'll just *say*, 'Tommy and Annika, now it's time to go back to Villa Villekulla.' "

Annika raised her head from the table and Tommy said, "What do you mean by that?"

"What do I mean!" said Pippi. "Don't you understand plain words? Or have I forgotten to tell you that you're coming along to Kurrekurredutt Island? I thought I'd mentioned it."

Tommy and Annika jumped to their feet. Their breath came in gasps. Then Tommy said, "You talk such nonsense! Our mother and father would never allow it."

"Yes, they will," said Pippi. "I've already talked to your mother."

For exactly five seconds there was silence in the kitchen of Villa Villekulla. Then there were two piercing yells from Tommy and Annika, who were wild with joy. Mr. Nilsson, who was sitting on the table and trying to spread butter on his hat, looked up in surprise. He was still more surprised when he saw Pippi and Tommy and Annika take one another by the hand and start dancing crazily around. They danced and shouted so that the ceiling lamp loosened and fell down. Then Mr. Nilsson threw the butter knife out the window and started to dance too.

"Is it really, really true?" asked Tommy when they had calmed down and crawled into the wood-bin to talk it over. Pippi nodded.

Yes, it was really true. Tommy and Annika were to go along to Kurrekurredutt Island.

To be sure, all the ladies in the little town came to Mrs. Settergren and said, "You don't mean that you're thinking of sending your children off to the South Seas with Pippi Longstocking? You can't be serious!"

Then Mrs. Settergren said, "And why shouldn't I? The children have been sick and the doctor says they need a change of climate. As long as I've known Pippi she has never done anything that has harmed Tommy and Annika in any way. No one can be kinder to them than she."

"Yes, but after all, *Pippi Longstocking*," said the ladies, wrinkling their noses.

"Exactly," said Mrs. Settergren. "Pippi Longstocking's manners may not always be what they ought to. But her heart is in the right place."

On a chilly night in early spring Tommy and Annika left the little town for the first time in their lives to travel out into the great, strange world with Pippi. All three of them were standing at the rail of the *Hoptoad* while the brisk night air filled the sails. (Perhaps it would be more accurate to say all five, because the horse and Mr. Nilsson were there too.)

All the children's classmates were on the pier and almost in tears with regret—mingled with envy— at their leaving. Tomorrow the classmates would be going to school as usual. Their geography homework was to study all the islands in the South Pacific. Tommy and Annika didn't have to do any homework for a while. "Their health comes before school," the doctor had said. "And they'll get to know the South Sea islands first hand," added Pippi.

Tommy's and Annika's mother and father were also on the pier. Tommy and Annika suddenly felt lumps in their throats when they saw their parents wiping their eyes with handkerchiefs. But Tommy and Annika still couldn't keep from being happy, so happy that it almost hurt.

Slowly the *Hoptoad* sailed out of the harbor.

"Tommy and Annika," cried Mrs. Settergren,

"when you get out on the North Sea you have to put on two undershirts and—"

The rest of what she was trying to say was drowned in the cries of farewell from the people on the pier, the wild whinnying of the horse, Pippi's happy noisiness, and Captain Longstocking's loud trumpeting when he blew his nose.

The voyage had begun. The *Hoptoad* was sailing out under the stars. Ice blocks were floating around the bow and the wind was singing in the sails.

"Oh, Pippi," said Annika, "I have such a funny feeling. I'm beginning to think that I'll be a pirate too when I grow up."

7
Pippi Goes Ashore

"Kurrekurredutt Island straight ahead!" cried Pippi from the bridge one sunny morning.

They had been sailing for days and nights, for weeks and months, over storm-ridden seas and through calm, friendly waters, in starlight and moonlight, under dark, threatening skies and in scorching sun. They had been sailing for such a long time that Tommy and Annika had almost forgotten what it was like to live at home in the little town.

Their mother would probably have been surprised if she could have seen them now. No more pale cheeks. Brown and healthy, they climbed around in the rigging just as Pippi did. Gradually, as the weather grew warmer, they had peeled off their clothes and the warmly bundled-up children with two undershirts who had crossed the North Sea had become two naked brown children in loincloths.

"What a wonderful time we're having!" Tommy and Annika declared each morning when they woke up in the cabin they shared with Pippi.

Often Pippi was already up and at the helm.

"A better seaman than my daughter has never sailed on the seven seas," Captain Longstocking would often say. And he was right. Pippi guided the *Hoptoad* with a sure hand past the most perilous underwater reefs and the worst breakers.

Now the voyage was coming to an end.

"Kurrekurredutt Island straight ahead!" cried Pippi.

There it was, sheltered by green palms and surrounded by the bluest blue water.

Two hours later the *Hoptoad* made for a little inlet on the left side of the island. All the Kurrekurredutts, men, women, and children, were on the beach to receive their king and his redheaded daughter. A mighty roar rose from the crowd when the gangplank was lowered.

"*Ussamkura, kussomkara!*" they shouted, and it meant, "Welcome back, fat white chief!"

King Efraim walked majestically down the gangplank, dressed in his blue corduroy suit, while on the foredeck, Fridolf played the new national anthem of the Kurrekurredutts on his accordion. "Here comes our chief with a clang and a bang!"

King Efraim raised his hand in greeting and shouted, *"Muoni manana!"* That meant, "Greetings to all of you."

He was followed by Pippi, who was carrying the horse. Then a wave of excitement broke out among the Kurrekurredutts. Of course they had heard about Pippi and her enormous strength, but it was something entirely different to see it before their very eyes. Tommy and Annika and the whole crew trooped ashore, but for the time being the Kurrekurredutts had eyes for no one but Pippi. Captain Longstocking lifted her up on his shoulders so that they would be able to have a good look at her, and again an excited murmur went through the crowd. But then Pippi lifted up Captain Longstocking on one of *her* shoulders and the horse on the other and the murmur swelled into a roar.

The population of the Island of Kurrekurredutt was one hundred and twenty-six people.

"That is approximately the right number of subjects to have," said King Efraim. "More are hard to keep track of."

They all lived in small, cozy huts among the palms. The biggest and finest hut belonged to King Efraim. The crew of the *Hoptoad* also had their huts where they lived while the ship lay anchored in the little inlet. She was anchored there practically all the time these days. Once in a while, though, there would be an expedition to an island about fifty miles to the north where there was a shop where Captain Longstocking bought snuff.

A fine, newly built little hut under a cocoanut tree was ready for Pippi. There was plenty of room for Tommy and Annika too. But before they could go into the hut to wash up, Captain Longstocking wanted to show them something. He took Pippi by the arm and led her back down to the beach.

"Here," he said, pointing with a thick forefinger. "This was the place where I floated ashore the time I was blown into the sea."

The Kurrekurredutts had put up a monument to commemorate the strange event. The stone bore an inscription which read, in Kurrekurredutt words:

Over the great wide sea came our fat white chief. This is the place where he floated ashore at the time when the breadfruit trees were in bloom. May he remain just as fat and magnificent as when he came.

In a voice trembling with emotion Captain Longstocking read the inscription out loud for Pippi and Tommy and Annika. Then he blew his nose with gusto.

When the sun had begun to go down and was

ready to disappear in the endless embrace of the
South Seas, the drums of the Kurrekurredutts sum-
moned everyone to the royal square, which was sit-
uated in the middle of the village. There stood King
Efraim's fine throne of bamboo, bedecked with red
hibiscus flowers. He sat on it when he ruled. For
Pippi the Kurrekurredutts had made a smaller
throne which stood next to her father's. In a great
hurry they had also put together two little bamboo
chairs for Tommy and Annika.

The roar of the drums grew louder and louder as
King Efraim mounted his throne with great dignity.
He had taken off his corduroy suit and was dressed
in royal regalia, with a crown on his head, a straw
skirt around his waist, a necklace of shark's teeth
around his neck, and heavy bracelets around his an-
kles. With great majesty, Pippi took her place on her
throne. She was still wearing the same loincloth
around her middle, but she had stuck some red and
white flowers in her hair to be a bit more festive.
Annika had done the same. But not Tommy. Nothing could make Tommy stick flowers in his hair.

King Efraim had been away from his ruling du-
ties for quite a while, and now he started to rule
with all his might. In the meantime the little Kurrekurredutt children came closer and closer to Pippi's
throne. They were filled with awe to think that she

was a princess. When they reached the throne they all threw themselves down on their knees before her, touching the ground with their foreheads.

Pippi quickly hopped down from her throne. "What's all this?" she asked. "Do you play 'hunting-for-treasure' down here too? Wait and let me play with you." She got down on her knees and started to nose around on the ground. "There seem to have been other treasure hunters here before us," she said after a while. "There isn't as much as a pin here, that's for sure."

She got back up on her throne. Hardly had she sat down when all the children bowed their heads to the ground again.

"Have you lost something?" said Pippi. "In any case it isn't there, so you might as well get up."

Luckily Captain Longstocking had been on the island long enough for the Kurrekurredutts to learn some of his language. Naturally they didn't know the meaning of such difficult words as "postal money order" and "brigadier general," but they had picked up a lot just the same. Even the children knew the most common expressions, such as "leave that alone" and similar ones. A little boy by the name of Momo could speak the Captain's language quite well, because he used to spend a good deal of time at the huts of the crew, listening to the men

talking. A pretty little girl named Moana was also able to understand the language quite well.

Now Momo was trying to explain to Pippi why they were on their knees in front of her.

"You be very fine princess," he said.

"I no be very fine princess," said Pippi in broken Kurrekurredutt. "I be really only Pippi Longstocking, and now I'm through with this throne business."

She hopped down off her throne. And King Efraim hopped down off his, because now he was finished with ruling for the day.

The sun sank like a red ball of fire in the South Seas and soon the sky was bright with stars. The Kurrekurredutts lighted a huge fire in the royal square, and King Efraim and Pippi and Tommy and Annika and the crew from the *Hoptoad* sat down in the grass and watched the Kurrekurredutts dance around the fire. The muffled rumble of the drums, the exciting dance, the strange perfumes from thousands of exotic flowers in the jungle, the glimmering stars above their heads—everything made Tommy and Annika feel very strange. The waves of the sea were ceaselessly pounding in the background.

"I think that this is a very fine island," said Tommy afterward, when he and Pippi and Annika had crawled into their beds in their cozy little hut under the cocoanut tree.

"I think so too," said Annika. "Don't you, Pippi?"

Pippi was lying there quietly with her feet on her pillow as was her habit. "M-m-m," she said dreamily. "Just listen to the roar of the waves. Remember, I said, 'Maybe I'll like it so much on Kurrekurredutt Island that I'll feel like staying there forever'?"

8
Pippi
Talks Sense
to a Shark

Very early the next morning Pippi and Tommy and
Annika crawled out of their hut. But the Kurrekurredutt children had been up still earlier. They were
already sitting under the cocoanut tree, excitedly
waiting for their new friends to come out and play.
They talked in rapid Kurrekurredutt and laughed,
their teeth flashing.

The whole crowd trooped down to the beach, with
Pippi at the head. Tommy and Annika jumped up
and down with delight when they saw the beautiful
white sand where they could dig themselves down,
and the blue sea, which looked so inviting. A coral
reef a short distance from the island served as a sea
wall. Inside, the water lay still and mirror-like. All
the children threw off their scanty clothing and,
shouting and laughing, dashed out into the water.

Afterward they rolled around in the white sand
and Pippi and Tommy and Annika agreed that it

would have been much nicer to have really dark
skin because white sand on a dark background
looked so funny. But when Pippi had dug herself
down in the sand up to her neck, so that only a
freckled face and two red pigtails stuck out, that
looked quite funny too. All the children settled themselves down in a circle to talk to her.

"Tell us about the children in the northern land
you come from," said Momo to the freckled face.

"They love pluttification," said Pippi.

"It's called *multiplication*," said Annika. "And
besides," she said, somewhat miffed, "no one can
say that we *love* it."

"Northern children love pluttification," Pippi insisted stubbornly. "Northern children become fran-
tic if northern children don't every day get a large
dose of pluttification."

She didn't have the strength to continue in broken
Kurrekurredutt, but switched over to her own language.

"If you hear a northern child cry, you can be sure
that the school has burned down or that a school
holiday has been declared or that the teacher has
forgotten to give the children homework in pluttification. And let's not even talk about the summer
vacation. That brings on such tears and wailing that
you wish you were dead when you hear it. No one

is dry-eyed when the school gate slams shut for the summer. All the children slowly head for home, singing sad songs, and they can't keep themselves from sobbing when they think that it will be several months before they can get any pluttification to do again. Yes, it's a misery, the like of which you can't imagine," said Pippi and sighed deeply.

"Bah!" said Tommy and Annika.

Momo didn't quite understand what pluttification was and wanted to have a more detailed explanation. Tommy was just about to explain it, but Pippi got in ahead of him.

"Yes, you see, it's like this—seven times seven equals a hundred and two. Fun, eh?"

"It most certainly is *not* one hundred and two," said Annika.

"No, because seven times seven is forty-nine," said Tommy.

"Remember that we're on Kurrekurredutt Island now," said Pippi. "Here we have an entirely different and much more flourishing climate, so seven times seven gets to be much more here."

"Bah!" said Tommy and Annika again.

The arithmetic lesson was interrupted by Captain Longstocking, who came to announce that he and the whole crew and all the Kurrekurredutts were going off to another island for a couple of days to hunt wild boar. Captain Longstocking was in the mood for some fresh boar steak. The Kurrekurredutt women were also to go along, to scare out the boar with wild cries. That meant that the children would be staying behind alone on the island.

"I hope you won't be sad because of this?" said Captain Longstocking.

"I'll give you three guesses," said Pippi. "The day I hear that some children are sad because they have to take care of themselves without grownups, that day I'll learn the whole pluttification table backward, I'll swear to that."

"That's my girl," said Captain Longstocking.

Then he and all his grown-up subjects armed with shields and arrows got into their big canoes and paddled away from Kurrekurredutt Island.

Pippi rounded her hands into a megaphone and shouted after them, "May peace be with you! But if you aren't back by my fiftieth birthday I'll send out an S.O.S. over the radio!"

When they were alone Pippi and Tommy and Annika and Momo and Moana and all the other children looked happily at one another. They were going to have a whole wonderful South Sea island all to themselves for several days.

"What are we going to do?" said Tommy and Annika.

"First we'll get our breakfast down from the trees," said Pippi. Like a flash she was in a cocoanut tree, shaking cocoanuts down. Momo and the other Kurrekurredutt children gathered breadfruit and bananas. Pippi made a fire on the beach and over it she roasted the wonderful breadfruit. All the children settled around in a circle and had a substantial breakfast consisting of roasted breadfruit, cocoanut milk, and bananas.

There were no horses on Kurrekurredutt Island, so all the native children were very much interested in Pippi's horse. Those who dared went for a ride on him. Moana said that one day she would like to go to the northern land where there were such strange animals.

Mr. Nilsson wasn't anywhere in evidence. He had gone off on an excursion to the jungle, where he had met some relatives.

"What are we going to do now?" asked Tommy and Annika when riding on the horse was no longer any fun.

"Northern children want to see fine caves—yes? —no?" wondered Momo.

"Northern children most certainly want to see fine caves—yes, yes," said Pippi.

Kurrekurredutt Island was a coral island. On the south side the high coral cliffs plunged straight into the sea, and there were the most wonderful caves which had been dug out by the waves. Some were down at the water line and filled with water, but there were others higher up in the cliffs and there the Kurrekurredutt children were accustomed to play. In the largest cave they kept a big supply of cocoanuts and other delicacies. To get there was quite an undertaking. First they had to climb carefully down the steep side of the cliff and hang on to the rocks which jutted out. Otherwise they could easily have plunged down into the sea. Any place else on the island that wouldn't have mattered. But at this particular spot there were plenty of sharks who liked to eat little children. In spite of this danger, the Kurrekurredutt children had fun diving for oysters, but then someone always had to stand guard and shout "Shark! Shark!" as soon as they spotted a fin in the distance.

In the big cave the Kurrekurredutt children also kept a supply of shimmering pearls which they had found in the oysters. They used them to play marbles with and they had no idea that they would be worth any amount of money in Europe or America. Captain Longstocking used to take along a few pearls now and then when he went off to buy snuff. He would trade the pearls for things he thought his subjects needed, but on the whole he felt that the

Kurrekurredutts were well off as they were. And the children gaily continued to play marbles with the pearls.

Annika was horror-stricken when Tommy said to her that she would have to climb along the cliff to the big cave. The first part wasn't so bad. There was quite a broad ledge to walk on, but it gradually got narrower and the last few feet to the cave you had to scramble and climb and hang on as best you could.

"Never!" said Annika. "Never."

To climb along a cliff where there was hardly anything to hold on to, and below, a sea filled with sharks waiting for you to fall down! That wasn't Annika's idea of fun.

Tommy was annoyed. "No one should bring sisters along to the South Seas," he said as he scrambled along the cliff wall. "Look at me! You only have to go like this—"

There was a loud *plop,* as Tommy fell into the water. Annika screamed. Even the Kurrekurredutt children were terrified. "Shark! Shark!" they cried and pointed out toward the sea. There a fin was clearly visible above the surface, heading rapidly in the direction of Tommy.

There was another *plop.* That was Pippi jumping in. She reached Tommy about the same time as the shark did. Terrified, Tommy was screaming at the top of his lungs. He felt the shark's sharp teeth scrape against his leg. But just at that instant Pippi grabbed the bloodthirsty beast with both hands and lifted him out of the water.

"Don't you have any shame in you?" she asked. The shark looked around, surprised and ill at ease. He wasn't able to breathe above the surface.

"Promise never to do that again and I'll let you go," said Pippi gravely. With all her force she flung him far out into the sea. He lost no time in getting away from there and decided to head for the Atlantic Ocean.

In the meantime Tommy had managed to scramble up on a small plateau, and he sat there trembling all over. His leg was bleeding. Then Pippi came up. She behaved very strangely. First she lifted Tommy up in the air, and then she hugged him so hard that he lost his breath. Then all of a sudden she let go of him and sat down on the cliff. She put her head in her hands. She cried. Pippi cried! Tommy and Annika and all the Kurrekurredutt children looked at her, surprised and frightened.

"You cry because Tommy almost eaten up?" said Momo.

"No," Pippi answered crossly, and wiped her eyes. "I cry because poor little hungry shark no get breakfast today."

9
Pippi
Talks Sense
to Jim and Buck

The shark's teeth had only scratched Tommy's leg, and when he had calmed down he still wanted to continue the climb to the big cave. Pippi twisted strands of hibiscus fiber into a stout rope and tied it to a stone. Then, lightly as a mountain goat, she hopped over to the cave and secured the other end of the rope there. Now even Annika dared to climb to the cave. When you had a steady rope to hang on to, it was easy.

It was a wonderful cave, and so big that all the children were able to get inside without any trouble.

"This cave is almost better than our hollow oak at Villa Villekulla," said Tommy.

"No, not better, but just as good," said Annika, who felt a lump in her throat at the thought of the oak and didn't want to admit that anything could be better.

Momo showed the visitors how much cocoanut

and breadfruit were stored in the cave. One would be able to live there for several weeks without starving to death. Moana showed them a hollow bamboo cane filled with the most beautiful pearls. She gave Pippi and Tommy and Annika each a handful.

"Nice marbles you have to play marbles with in this country," said Pippi.

It was delightful to sit at the opening of the cave and look out over the sea glittering in the sunlight. And it was great fun to lie on one's tummy and spit into the water. Tommy announced a contest in long-distance spitting. Momo was terribly good at it. But he still wasn't able to beat Pippi. She had a way of forcing the spit through her front teeth which no one could imitate.

"If it's drizzling over in New Zealand today," said Pippi, "it's my fault."

Tommy and Annika didn't do so well.

"Northern children no can spit," said Momo with a superior air. He didn't quite consider Pippi as being one of the northern children.

"So northern children can't spit?" said Pippi. "You don't know what you're talking about. That is taught to them in school from the first grade. Long-distance spitting and altitude spitting and sprint spitting. You ought to see Tommy's and Annika's teacher! Man, can she spit! She won first prize in sprint spitting. The whole town cheers when she runs around spitting to beat the band."

"Bah!" said Tommy and Annika.

Pippi raised her hand to shield her eyes from the glare and looked out to sea. "I see a ship out there," she said. "A tiny steamer. I wonder what it's doing in these parts."

And she had reason to wonder!

The steamer was heading toward Kurrekurredutt Island at a good clip. On board there were several South Sea islanders and two white men. Their names were Jim and Buck. They were dirty, coarse-looking men who looked like real bandits. And that is exactly what they were.

Once when Captain Longstocking was in the shop where he bought snuff, Jim and Buck had been there too. They had seen Captain Longstocking put a couple of unusually large and beautiful pearls on the counter and had heard him say that on Kurrekurredutt Island the children used pearls like these to play marbles with. Since that day they had only one goal and that was to go to the island and try to get pearls. They knew that Captain Longstocking was very strong, and they also had a healthy respect for the crew of the *Hoptoad*. They therefore decided to take advantage of an opportunity when all the men were away on a hunt.

Now their chance had come. Hiding behind an island close by, they had seen through their binoculars Captain Longstocking, his crew, and all the Kurrekurredutts paddle away from the island. They were only waiting until the canoes were out of sight.

"Drop the anchor!" shouted Buck when the ship was close to the island. Pippi and all the other children watched them in silence from the cave above. The men dropped anchor, and Jim and Buck jumped into a skiff and rowed ashore. The crew were given orders to stay on board.

"Now we'll sneak up to the village and overtake them," said Jim. "Probably only the women and children are at home."

"Yes," said Buck, "and besides, there were so many women in the canoes I should think that only children are left on the island. I hope they're playing marbles—ha-ha-ha!" His voice carried clearly over the water.

"Why?" shouted Pippi from the cave. "Do you especially like playing marbles? I think it's just as much fun to play leapfrog."

Jim and Buck turned around in astonishment and saw Pippi and all the children sticking their heads out from the cave. A delighted grin spread over their faces.

"There we have the kids," said Jim.

"Perfect," said Buck. "This is in the bag."

But they decided nevertheless to play it safe and be sly. No one could know where the children kept their pearls, and therefore it was best to try to win them over. The men pretended that they hadn't come to Kurrekurredutt Island to find pearls at all, but were just out for a nice little excursion. They felt hot and sticky, and Buck suggested that, to begin with, they go for a swim.

"I'll row back to the boat and fetch our bathing trunks," he said. This he did. In the meantime Jim stood alone on the shore.

"Is there a good beach around here?" he called to the children in a friendly voice.

"Wonderful," said Pippi. "Absolutely wonderful for sharks. They come here every day."

"Nonsense," said Jim. "I don't see any sharks."

But he was a little worried just the same. When Buck came back with the bathing trunks, Jim told him what Pippi had said.

"Nonsense," said Buck, and he shouted to Pippi, "Are you the one who is saying that it's dangerous to swim here?"

"No," said Pippi, "I never said that."

"That's funny," said Jim. "Didn't you just tell me that there were sharks here?"

"Yes, that's what I said. But dangerous—no, that I wouldn't say exactly. My grandfather swam here last year."

"Well, then," said Buck.

"And Grandfather got back from the hospital already last Friday," Pippi went on, "with the fanciest wooden leg you've ever seen on an old man." She spat thoughtfully into the water. "So I couldn't really say that it's dangerous. Of course a few arms and legs do disappear if one swims here. But as long as wooden legs don't cost more than a dollar a pair I don't think you should deprive yourself of an invigorating swim just because of miserliness." She spat once more.

"My grandfather takes a childish delight in his wooden leg. He says it is absolutely irreplaceable when he goes out to fight."

"You know what I think," said Buck. "I think you're telling whoppers. Your grandfather must be an old man. I'm sure he doesn't want to be in any fights."

"That's what you think!" cried Pippi in a shrill voice. "He's the most ill-tempered old man who ever hit his opponent on the head with a wooden leg. If he can't fight from morning till night he's miserable. Then he gets into such a rage that he bites himself on the nose."

"What nonsense!" said Buck. "No one can bite himself on the nose."

"Yes, they can," Pippi insisted. "He climbs up on a chair."

Buck thought about this for a while, but then he swore. "I don't feel like listening to your silly chatter any longer. Come on, Jim, let's get undressed."

"Besides, I'd like to have you know that my grandfather has the longest nose in the world. He has five parrots and all of them can sit next to each other on his nose."

By now Buck was really angry. "You little redheaded vixen, do you know that you're the worst liar I've ever met? Aren't you ashamed of yourself? Are you really trying to make me believe that five parrots can sit in a row on your grandfather's nose? Confess that it's a lie!"

"Yes," said Pippi sadly. "It's a lie."

"There, you see," said Buck. "Isn't that what I said?"

"It's a terrible, horrible lie," said Pippi, still sadder.

"That's what I thought from the beginning," said Buck.

"Because the fifth parrot," sobbed Pippi and burst out into a flood of tears, "the fifth parrot has to stand on one leg."

"Get lost," said Buck, and he and Jim went behind a bush to get undressed.

"Pippi, you don't even have a grandfather," said Annika reproachfully.

"No," said Pippi gaily, "*must* I have a grandfather?"

Buck was the first one to come out in his bathing trunks. He made an elegant dive from a cliff into the sea and swam out. The children up in the cave watched with great interest. Then they spotted a shark fin, which flashed above the surface of the water for a second.

"Shark, shark!" cried Momo.

Buck, who was treading water and enjoying himself immensely, turned around and saw the terrible creature coming toward him.

There has probably never been anyone who could swim as fast as Buck swam then. In two split seconds he had reached shore and rushed out of the water. He was both frightened and furious, and it seemed as if he thought it was all Pippi's fault that there were sharks in the water.

"Aren't you ashamed of yourself, you nasty brat?" he screamed. "The sea is full of sharks."

"Have I said anything else?" Pippi asked sweetly, and tilted her head to one side. "I don't always lie, you see."

Jim and Buck went behind the bush to get dressed again. They felt that now the time had come to begin thinking about the pearls. No one could tell how long Captain Longstocking and the others were going to be away.

"Listen, children," said Buck. "I heard someone say that there were some good oyster beds in these regions. Do you know if it's true?"

"I'll say," said Pippi. "Oyster shells go crunch-crunch under your feet wherever you walk down there on the bottom of the sea. Go down and see for yourself."

But Buck didn't want to do that.

"There are great big pearls in every oyster," said Pippi. "About like this one." She held up a giant, shimmering pearl.

Jim and Buck got so excited that they could hardly stand still.

"Do you have any more of those?" said Jim. "We would like to buy them from you."

This was a lie. Jim and Buck had no money with which to buy pearls. They only wanted to get them dishonestly.

"Yes, we have at least ten or twelve quarts of pearls here in the cave," said Pippi.

Jim and Buck were unable to hide their delight.

"Wonderful," said Buck. "Bring them here and we'll buy them all."

"Oh no," said Pippi. "What are the poor children going to use to play marbles with afterward? Have you thought of that?"

There was a lot of discussion back and forth before Jim and Buck realized that it would be impossible to get the pearls by clever maneuvering. But what they couldn't get by clever maneuvering, they decided to take by force. Now they at least knew where the pearls were. The only thing they had to do was climb over to the cave and take them.

Climb over to the cave—yes, that was the rub. During the discussion Pippi had carefully removed the hibiscus rope, which was now safely in the cave.

Jim and Buck didn't think that the climb over to the cave looked very inviting. But there didn't seem to be any other way to get the pearls.

"You do it, Jim," said Buck.

"No, you do it, Buck," said Jim.

"*You do it, Jim,*" said Buck. He was stronger than Jim. So Jim started climbing. He frantically grabbed hold of all the jutting rocks he could reach. Cold sweat was pouring down his back.

"Hold on, for heaven's sake, so you won't fall down," said Pippi in an encouraging way.

Then Jim fell in. Buck was shouting and cursing on the beach. Jim was also screaming because he saw two sharks heading in his direction. When they were no more than three feet from him, Pippi threw down a cocoanut right in front of their snouts. That scared them just long enough for Jim to swim to the shore and crawl up on the little plateau. The water was running in rivulets from his clothes and he looked miserable. Buck was scolding him.

"Do it yourself, and you'll see how easy it is," said Jim.

"Now *I'll* show you how," said Buck and started to climb.

All the children watched him. Annika was almost a bit frightened as she watched him coming closer.

"Oh-oh, don't climb there, you'll fall in," said Pippi.

"Where?" said Buck.

"There," said Pippi, pointing. Buck looked down.

"A lot of cocoanuts get wasted this way," said Pippi a moment later when she had thrown one in the sea to prevent the sharks from eating up Buck, who was desperately floundering in the water. But up he came, mad as a hornet, and he certainly wasn't one to be afraid. He immediately started climbing again, because he had made up his mind once and for all to make his way into the cave and get his hands on the pearls.

This time he managed much better. When he was

almost at the opening of the cave he called out triumphantly, "Now, you little demons, this time you're going to get it."

Then Pippi stuck out her index finger and poked him in the stomach.

There was a splash.

"You could at least have taken this with you when you took off!" Pippi shouted after him as she landed a cocoanut bang on the snout of a shark that was coming too close. But more sharks came and she had to throw more cocoanuts. One of them hit Buck on the head.

"Oh dear, was that you?" said Pippi when Buck yelled. "From up here you look like a big, nasty shark."

Jim and Buck now decided to sit it out until the children were forced to come down.

"When they get hungry they'll leave there," said Buck grimly. "And then they'll see something." He shouted to the children, "I feel sorry for you if you're going to have to sit in that cave until you starve to death!"

"You have a kind heart," said Pippi, "but you won't have to worry about us for the next two weeks. Then we might have to start rationing the cocoanuts a little."

She cracked a big cocoanut, drank the milk, and ate the wonderful meat.

Jim and Buck swore. The sun was setting and they began making preparations to spend the night ashore. They didn't dare row out to the steamer to sleep because then the children could get away with all the pearls. They lay down on the hard rocks in their wet clothes. They were very uncomfortable.

Up in the cave all the children were merrily sitting and eating cocoanuts and mashed breadfruit. It was so good. The whole situation was so exciting and pleasant. Once in a while they would stick their heads out to look at Jim and Buck. By now it was so dark that they could see only a fuzzy outline of the men on the plateau below. But they could still hear them swearing down there.

Suddenly there was a shower of the violent tropical kind. The rain came down in torrents. Pippi stuck the tip of her nose out of the cave. "You certainly are the lucky ones!" she shouted to Jim and Buck.

"What do you mean by that?" said Buck hopefully. He thought that the children had perhaps changed their minds and wanted to give them the pearls. "What do you mean by saying we're lucky?"

"I mean, just think how lucky it is that you were

already soaked before this rainstorm came. Otherwise you would have got soaking wet in this rain."

More swearing could be heard from down on the plateau, but it was impossible to tell whether it was Jim or Buck.

"Good night, and sleep well," said Pippi. "Because that's what we're going to do now."

The children lay down on the floor of the cave. Tommy and Annika lay one on either side of Pippi, holding her hands. They were quite comfortable. It was so warm and snug in the cave. Outside the rain was pouring down.

10
Pippi
Gets Bored
with Jim and Buck

The children slept soundly all night. But Jim and Buck did not. They kept on grumbling about the rain, and when it stopped they started to argue about whose fault it was that they hadn't been able to get hold of the pearls and which one of them had really had the stupid idea of going to Kurrekurredutt Island in the first place. And when the sun rose and dried their clothes, and Pippi's cheerful face popped out of the cave, saying good morning, they were more determined than ever to get the pearls and leave the island as rich men. But they couldn't figure out how to do it.

While all this was going on, Pippi's horse had begun to wonder where Pippi and Tommy and Annika had disappeared to. Mr. Nilsson had returned from his family reunion in the jungle and he was wondering the same thing. He also wondered what Pippi would say when she found out that he had lost his straw hat.

Mr. Nilsson jumped up on the horse's tail and the horse trotted off to find Pippi. Finally he found his way to the south side of the island. That is where he saw Pippi stick her head out of the cave, and he whinnied happily.

"Look, Pippi, there's your horse!" cried Tommy.

"And Mr. Nilsson is sitting on his tail," said Annika.

Jim and Buck heard this. They realized that the horse who was trotting along the beach belonged to Pippi, the redheaded girl up in the cave.

Buck went and grabbed the horse by the mane.

"Now listen, you little monster," he shouted to Pippi, "I'm going to kill your horse!"

"You're going to kill my horse whom I love so dearly?" said Pippi. "My nice, good horse! You can't mean it."

"Yes, I'll probably have to," said Buck. "That is, if you don't want to come here and give us all the pearls. All of them, do you hear! Otherwise I'll kill the horse this instant."

Pippi looked at him gravely. "Please," she said. "I'm begging you—don't kill my horse, and do let the children keep their pearls."

"You heard me," Buck said. "Hand over the pearls this minute! Or else—"

And then in a low voice he said to Jim, "Just wait until she comes with the pearls. Then I'll beat her black and blue to pay her back for this miserable rainy night. As for the horse, we'll take him along on board and sell him on another island."

He shouted to Pippi, "Well, which is it going to be? Are you coming, or aren't you?"

"Yes, I'll come," said Pippi. "But don't forget that you asked for it."

She skipped along the projecting rocks as lightly as if she had been walking down a garden path and jumped down to the plateau. She stopped in front of Buck. There she stood, little and thin, with her two pigtails pointing straight out. There was a dangerous look in her eyes.

"Where are the pearls, you little beast?" shouted Buck.

"There aren't going to be any pearls today. You'll have to play leapfrog instead."

Then Buck let out a roar which made Annika tremble way up in the cave. "I'm going to kill both you and the horse!" he yelled as he lunged toward Pippi.

"Take it easy, my good man," said Pippi. She

grabbed him around the waist and threw him ten feet up in the air. He banged himself quite hard on the rocks as he came down. Then Jim came to life. He raised his arm to give Pippi a terrible blow, but she jumped aside with a little chuckle. A second later Jim was also on his way up into the clear morning sky. There they sat, Jim and Buck, on the rock, groaning. Pippi walked up and grabbed them, one in each fist.

"You *can't* be as anxious to play marbles as you seem to be," she said. "There has to be some limit to your playfulness." She carried them down to the skiff and tossed them in.

"Now you go home to your mothers and ask them to give you five cents for marbles," she said. "You'll find them just as easy to play with."

A little while later the steamer was chugging away from Kurrekurredutt Island. Since then it has never been seen in those waters.

Pippi patted her horse. Mr. Nilsson jumped up on her shoulder. Beyond the outermost tip of the island a whole row of canoes came into sight. It was Captain Longstocking and his people returning home after a successful hunt. Pippi shouted and waved at them and they waved back with their paddles.

Then Pippi quickly put up the rope again so that Tommy and Annika and the others could get down from the cave. And when the canoes came gliding in to the little inlet beside the *Hoptoad* a short time later, the whole crowd of children was there to greet them.

Captain Longstocking embraced Pippi. "Has everything been peaceful?" he asked.

"Oh, yes, completely peaceful," said Pippi.

"But Pippi, how can you say that?" said Annika. "We've had terrible things happen."

"Oh, yes, I forgot," said Pippi. "No, it hasn't been completely peaceful, Papa Efraim. As soon as you turn your back, things start to happen."

"But my dear child, what's happened?" said Captain Longstocking anxiously.

"Something really terrible," said Pippi. "Mr. Nilsson lost his straw hat."

11
Pippi Leaves Kurrekurredutt Island

Wonderful days followed—wonderful days in a warm, wonderful world full of sunshine, with the blue sea glittering and fragrant flowers everywhere.

Tommy and Annika were by now so brown that there was hardly any difference between them and the Kurrekurredutt children. And every spot on Pippi's face was covered with freckles.

"This trip will turn out to be a real beauty treatment for me," she said gaily. "I have more freckles and am therefore more beautiful than ever. If this keeps up, I shall be irresistible."

Momo and Moana and all the other Kurrekurredutt children already considered Pippi irresistible. They had never had such a good time before, and they were as fond of Pippi as Tommy and Annika were. Of course they were fond of Tommy and Annika too, and Tommy and Annika were fond of them. So they had a marvelous time together and played and played all day long. Often they would go up to the cave to play.

Pippi had taken blankets there, and when they wanted to they could spend the night and be even more comfortable than they were the first time. She had also made a rope ladder which reached all the way down to the water below the cave, and all the children climbed up and down on it and swam and splashed to their heart's delight. Now it was perfectly safe to swim. Pippi had blocked off a big section with net so that the sharks couldn't get in. It was such fun to swim in and out of those caves filled with water. Even Tommy and Annika had learned to dive for oysters. The first pearl that Annika found was a huge, beautiful pink one. She decided to take it home with her and have it made into a ring, which she would wear as a souvenir of Kurrekurredutt Island.

Sometimes they would play that Pippi was Buck trying to get into the cave to steal pearls. Then Tommy would pull up the rope ladder and Pippi would have to climb up the side of the cliff as best as she could. All the children would shout, "Buck is coming, Buck is coming!" when she stuck her head into the cave, and they would take turns at poking her in the stomach so that she tumbled backward into the sea. Down there she splashed around with her bare feet sticking out of the water, and the children laughed so hard that they almost fell out of the cave.

When they got tired of being in the cave they would play in their bamboo hut. Pippi and the children had built it, though of course Pippi had done most of the work. It was big and square and made of thin bamboo cane, and you could climb around inside it, and on top of it too. Next to the hut was a tall cocoanut tree. Pippi had hacked steps into it so that you could climb all the way to the top. The view was wonderful from up there. Between two other cocoanut palms Pippi had rigged up a swing of hibiscus fiber. It was marvelous, because if you swung as high as the swing would go, you could throw yourself out into the air and land in the water below.

Pippi swung so high and flew so far out into the water that she said, "One fine day I'll probably land in Australia, and then it won't be much fun for the one who gets me on the head."

The children also went on expeditions into the jungle. There was a high mountain and a waterfall that cascaded over a cliff. Pippi had made up her mind that she would like to go down the waterfall in a barrel. She brought along one of the barrels from the *Hoptoad* and crawled into it. Momo and

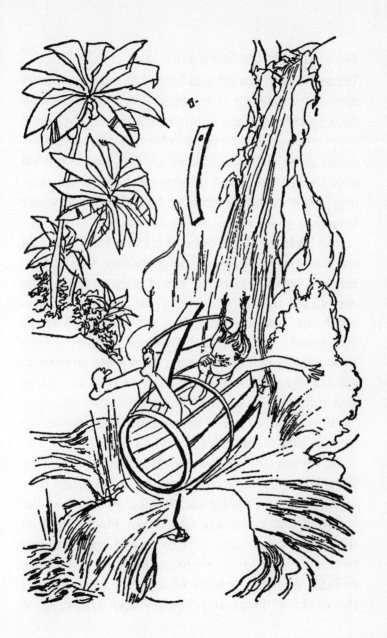

Tommy closed the lid and helped to push the barrel over the waterfall. It bounced down with tremendous speed and then it broke. All the children saw Pippi disappear into the tumbling water, and they didn't think they would ever see her again. But all of a sudden she dived up and climbed ashore, saying, "They certainly go at a fast clip, those water barrels."

The days went by. Soon the rainy season would start and then Captain Longstocking would lock himself into his hut and brood about life, and he was afraid that Pippi wouldn't be happy on Kurrekurredutt Island then. More often lately Tommy and Annika would find themselves wondering how their mother and father were. They were anxious to get home for Christmas. So they weren't as sad as you might expect when Pippi said one morning, "Tommy and Annika, how would you like to go back to Villa Villekulla for a while again?"

Of course, for Momo and Moana and the other Kurrekurredutt children it was a sad day when they saw Pippi and Tommy and Annika go on board the *Hoptoad* for the voyage home. But Pippi promised that they would come back often to Kurrekurredutt Island. The Kurrekurredutt children had made wreaths of white flowers which they hung around the necks of Pippi and Tommy and Annika as a farewell gesture. Their song of farewell sounded sad as it followed the ship out to sea.

Captain Longstocking was also standing on the beach. He had to stay behind in order to rule. Fridolf had taken it upon himself to get the children home. Captain Longstocking slowly and deliberately blew his nose in his big pocket handkerchief as he waved good-by. Pippi and Tommy and Annika cried, and the tears streamed down their faces as they waved to Captain Longstocking and the island children as long as they were in sight.

The *Hoptoad* had a fair wind behind her during the whole voyage home.

"We'd better dig out your undershirts in good time before we reach the North Sea," said Pippi.

"What an awful thought," said Tommy and Annika.

It soon became evident that despite the fair wind, the ship wouldn't reach home by Christmas. Tommy and Annika were bitterly disappointed when they heard it. Just think, no Christmas tree and no Christmas presents!

"Then we could just as well have stayed on Kurrekurredutt Island," said Tommy angrily.

Annika thought of her mother and father and knew that she would be glad to get home, no matter when. But it certainly was sad that they were going to miss Christmas. They both felt the same about that.

One dark night at the beginning of January, Pippi and Tommy and Annika spotted the lights of the little town from afar, twinkling a welcome. They were back home again.

"Well, now we have this trip behind us," said Pippi as she walked down the gangplank with her horse.

No one was at the port to meet them because no one had known when they would get home. Pippi lifted up Tommy and Annika and Mr. Nilsson onto the horse and they rode toward Villa Villekulla. The poor horse had a hard time. He had to plow his way through the snowdrifts piled up in the streets and roads. Tommy and Annika stared straight ahead into the snow flurry. Soon they would be back with their mother and father, and they were suddenly aware how much they had missed them.

In the Settergren house the lights were shining invitingly, and through the window they could see Tommy's and Annika's mother and father sitting at the dinner table.

"There are Mother and Father!" said Tommy and he sounded *so* happy and excited.

But Villa Villekulla lay in complete darkness and was covered with snow.

Annika was terribly unhappy at the thought of Pippi's going back there alone. "Please, Pippi, won't you stay with us the first night?" she asked.

"Oh, no," said Pippi and jumped down in the snow outside the gate. "I have to get some things in order at Villa Villekulla."

She waded through the deep snowdrifts which reached all the way up to her stomach. The horse plowed along behind her.

"Yes, but think of how cold it will be in there," said Tommy. "It hasn't been heated for such a long time."

"Nonsense," said Pippi. "If the heart is warm and beats the way it should, there is no reason to be cold."

12
Pippi Longstocking Doesn't Want to Grow Up

Oh, how Tommy's and Annika's mother and father hugged and kissed their children, and what a wonderful supper they prepared for them! Afterward they tucked them in, and sat for a long, long time on the edge of their beds, listening to the children's tales of all the strange things they had experienced on Kurrekurredutt Island. They were so happy, all of them. There was only one sad thing, and that was not having had any Christmas. Tommy and Annika didn't want to tell their mother how miserable they were because they had missed having a tree and presents, but that's the way it was. It seemed so strange to be back. It always does when you've been away, and it would have been much easier if they could have come home on Christmas Eve.

Tommy and Annika were also sad when they thought of Pippi. Now of course she would be home in bed at Villa Villekulla with her feet on her pillow, and there was no one there to tuck her in. They made up their minds to go to see her as soon as they could the next morning.

But the following day their mother didn't want to let them go because she hadn't seen them for such a long time, and besides, their grandmother was coming for dinner to welcome the children home. Tommy and Annika wondered anxiously what Pippi could be doing all day, and when it began to get dark they couldn't stand it any longer.

"Please, Mother, we have to go and see Pippi," said Tommy.

"Yes, run along then," said Mrs. Settergren. "But don't stay too long."

Tommy and Annika ran off.

When they got to the garden gate of Villa Ville-kulla they stopped and stared in amazement. It looked just like a Christmas card. The whole house was softly blanketed with snow and there were gleaming lights in all the windows. A torch was burning on the veranda and shedding its brightness over the snow-covered lawn. One path to the veranda was neatly shoveled, so Tommy and Annika didn't have to wade through the drifts.

Just as they were stamping the snow off their feet on the veranda, the door opened and there stood Pippi. "Merry Christmas!" she said.

She ushered them into the kitchen. And there was a Christmas tree! The lights were lit and seventeen sparklers were burning, filling the room with a nice smoky smell. The table was set with puddings and hams and sausages and all sorts of Christmas delicacies—yes, even gingerbread men and birds' nests. There was a fire in the stove, and the horse was standing at the woodbin, scraping his hoof in a very refined way. Mr. Nilsson was hopping back and forth among the sparklers in the Christmas tree.

"He is supposed to be an angel," said Pippi grimly, "but I can't get him to sit still."

Tommy and Annika just stood there, speechless.

"Oh, Pippi," said Annika finally, "how wonderful! When did you find time to do all this?"

"Me, I'm the hard-working type," said Pippi.

Tommy and Annika were suddenly overwhelmed with happiness.

"I think it's just grand to be back in Villa Villekulla again," said Tommy.

They sat down around the table and ate piles of ham and pudding and sausage and gingerbread men, and everything tasted even better to them than bananas and breadfruit.

"But Pippi, it isn't Christmas at all," said Tommy.

"Yes, sir," said Pippi. "The Villa Villekulla al-

manac is slow. I have to take it to an almanac-maker and have it adjusted so that it will run properly again."

"How wonderful," said Annika again. "We celebrated Christmas after all—except without Christmas presents, of course."

"That reminds me," said Pippi. "I have hidden your Christmas presents. You have to find them yourselves."

Tommy's and Annika's faces became flushed with excitement as they sprang up and started hunting. In the woodbin Tommy found a big package which was marked "TOMMY." Inside was a fine set of paints. Under the table Annika found a package with her name on it, and inside that was a pretty red parasol.

"I can take this with me to Kurrekurredutt Island the next time we go there," said Annika.

High up on the hood of the stove were two more packages. One contained a small jeep for Tommy, and in the other was a set of doll's dishes for Annika. A small package was also hanging on the horse's tail. In it was a clock for Tommy's and Annika's room.

When they had found all their Christmas presents, they gave Pippi big hugs and thanked her over and over again. She was standing at the kitchen window, looking out at all the snow in the garden.

"Tomorrow we'll build a big snow hut," she said. "And we'll have lights burning in it at night."

"Oh, yes, let's," said Annika, feeling happier than ever to be home.

"I'm wondering if we could make a ski slope running down from the roof to the snowdrifts below. I'm going to teach the horse to ski. But I can't decide whether he needs four skis or only two."

"We're going to have a wonderful time tomorrow," said Tommy. "What luck that we came home in the middle of Christmas vacation."

"We're always going to have fun," said Annika. "At Villa Villekulla, on Kurrekurredutt Island, and everywhere."

Pippi nodded in agreement. They had crawled up on the kitchen table, all three of them. Suddenly a dark shadow passed over Tommy's face.

"I never want to grow up," he said emphatically.

"I don't either," said Annika.

"No, that's nothing to wish for, being grown up," said Pippi. "Grownups never have any fun. They only have a lot of boring work and wear silly-looking clothes and have corns and minicipal taxes."

"It's called *municipal*," said Annika.

"Well, anyway, it's the same nonsense," said Pippi. "And then they're full of superstitions and all sorts of crazy things. They think that something terrible is going to happen if they happen to stick their knives in their mouths while they're eating, and things like that."

"And they can't play, either," said Annika.

"Ugh, how awful to have to grow up."

"Who says you have to grow up?" said Pippi. "If I remember right, I have a few pills somewhere."

"What sort of pills?" said Tommy.

"Some very fine pills for people who don't want to grow up," said Pippi and jumped down from the table. She hunted through closets and drawers and after a while she produced something that looked like three yellow peas.

"Peas!" said Tommy surprised.

"That's what you think," said Pippi. "These are no peas. They are chililug pills and were given to me in Rio by an old Indian chief when I happened to mention that I wasn't wild about the idea of growing up."

"You mean that those tiny little pills can do it?" said Annika skeptically.

"Absolutely," said Pippi. "But they have to be taken in the dark, and then you have to say this:

> *Pretty little chililug,*
> *I don't want to get bug.*

"You mean big," said Tommy.

"If I say 'bug' I mean 'bug,' " said Pippi. "That's the trick, you see. Most children say 'big,' and that's the worst thing that can happen. Because then you start to grow more then ever. Once there was a boy who ate pills like these. He said 'big' instead of 'bug' and he started growing until it was a nightmare—many, many feet every day. It was terrible. He was all right as long as he could go around grazing under the apple trees, the way a giraffe does. But then he got too big and that didn't work any longer. When some ladies came to visit and they wanted to say, 'My, what a nice big boy you've grown up to be,' they had to shout into a megaphone so that he would hear them. All you saw of him was his long, skinny legs disappearing up among the clouds like two flagpoles. He was never heard of after that—oh, yes, once he was. That was when he took a lick at the sun and got a blister on his tongue. Then he let out such a roar that the flowers down on earth wilted. But that was the last sign of life from him—although his legs are probably still wandering around down in Rio, making awful mix-ups in the traffic."

"Oh, I wouldn't dare eat one of those pills," said Annika, terrified, "in case I might say the wrong thing."

"You won't say the wrong thing," said Pippi reassuringly. "If I thought you'd do that, I wouldn't give you one. Because it would be boring to have just your legs to play with. Tommy and me and your legs—that would be fine company!"

"You won't make a mistake, Annika," said Tommy.

They turned the Christmas tree lights out. The kitchen was in complete darkness, except near the stove where the fire glowed behind the stove door.

They sat down in silence in a circle in the middle of the floor, holding one another by the hand. Pippi gave Tommy and Annika each a chililug pill. Chills ran up and down their spines. Just think, in a second the powerful pill would be down in their stomachs, and then they would never have to grow up. How marvelous that would be!

"Now," Pippi whispered.

"Pretty little chililug, I don't want to get big," they said all together and swallowed their pills. The deed was done.

Pippi turned on the ceiling light. "That's it," she said. "Now we don't have to be grown up and have corns and other miseries. Though the pills have been lying around in my closet for so long that one can't be absolutely sure that all the strength hasn't gone out of them. But we have to hope for the best."

Annika suddenly thought of something. "Oh,

Pippi," she said in alarm, "you were going to be a pirate when you grew up."

"Pshaw, I can be one anyway," said Pippi. "I can still become a nasty *little* pirate who spreads death and destruction around me."

She was quiet for a while, thinking. "Just imagine," she said. "If a lady walks by here one day many, many years from now and she sees us running around in the garden, perhaps she will ask Tommy, 'How old are you, my little friend?' And then you'll say, 'Fifty-three, if I'm not mistaken.'"

Tommy laughed merrily. "She'll probably think that I'm small for my age," he said.

"Of course," said Pippi. "But then you can explain that you were bigger when you were smaller."

Just then Annika and Tommy remembered that their mother had told them not to stay away too long.

"I think we'll have to go now," said Tommy.

"But we'll be back tomorrow," said Annika.

"Fine," said Pippi. "We'll get started on the snow hut at eight o'clock."

She walked with them to the gate and her red pigtails danced around her as she ran back to Villa Villekulla.

"You know," said Tommy a while later when he was brushing his teeth, "if I hadn't known that those were chililug pills I would have been willing to bet that they were just ordinary peas."

Annika was standing at the window of their room in her pink pajamas, looking over toward Villa Villekulla. "Look, I see Pippi!" she called out, delighted.

Tommy rushed over to the window too. Yes, there she was. Now that the trees didn't have any leaves they could look right into Pippi's kitchen.

Pippi was sitting at the table with her head propped against her arms. She was staring at the little flickering flame of a candle that was standing in front of her. She seemed to be dreaming.

"She—she looks so alone," said Annika, and her voice trembled a little. "Oh, Tommy, if it were only morning so that we could go to her right away!"

They stood there in silence and looked out into the winter night. The stars were shining over Villa Villekulla's roof. Pippi was inside. She would always be there. That was a comforting thought. The years would go by, but Pippi and Tommy and Annika would not grow up. That is, of course, if the strength hadn't gone out of the chililug pills. There would be new springs and summers, new autumns and winters, but their games would go on. Tomorrow they would build a snow hut and make a ski slope from the roof of Villa Villekulla, and when spring came they would climb the hollow oak where soda pop spouted up. They would hunt for treasure and they would ride Pippi's horse. They would sit in the woodbin and tell stories. Perhaps they would also take a trip to Kurrekurredutt Island now and then, to see Momo and Moana and the others. But they would always come back to Villa Villekulla.

And the most wonderful, comforting thought was that Pippi would always be in Villa Villekulla.

"If she would only look in this direction we could wave to her," said Tommy.

But Pippi continued to stare straight ahead with a dreamy look. Then she blew out the light.

ABOUT THE AUTHOR

Astrid Lindgren (1907-2002) was born in Sweden. After college, she worked in a newspaper office and a Swedish publishing house. *Pippi Longstocking* was originally published in Swedish in 1950, and was later translated into many other languages. It was followed by two sequels, *Pippi Goes on Board* (1957) and *Pippi in the South Seas* (1959). Astrid Lindgren was the first children's book writer to win the Peace Prize of the German Book Trade (1978). She also won the Hans Christian Andersen Medal (1958), the highest international award in children's literature. She had two children.